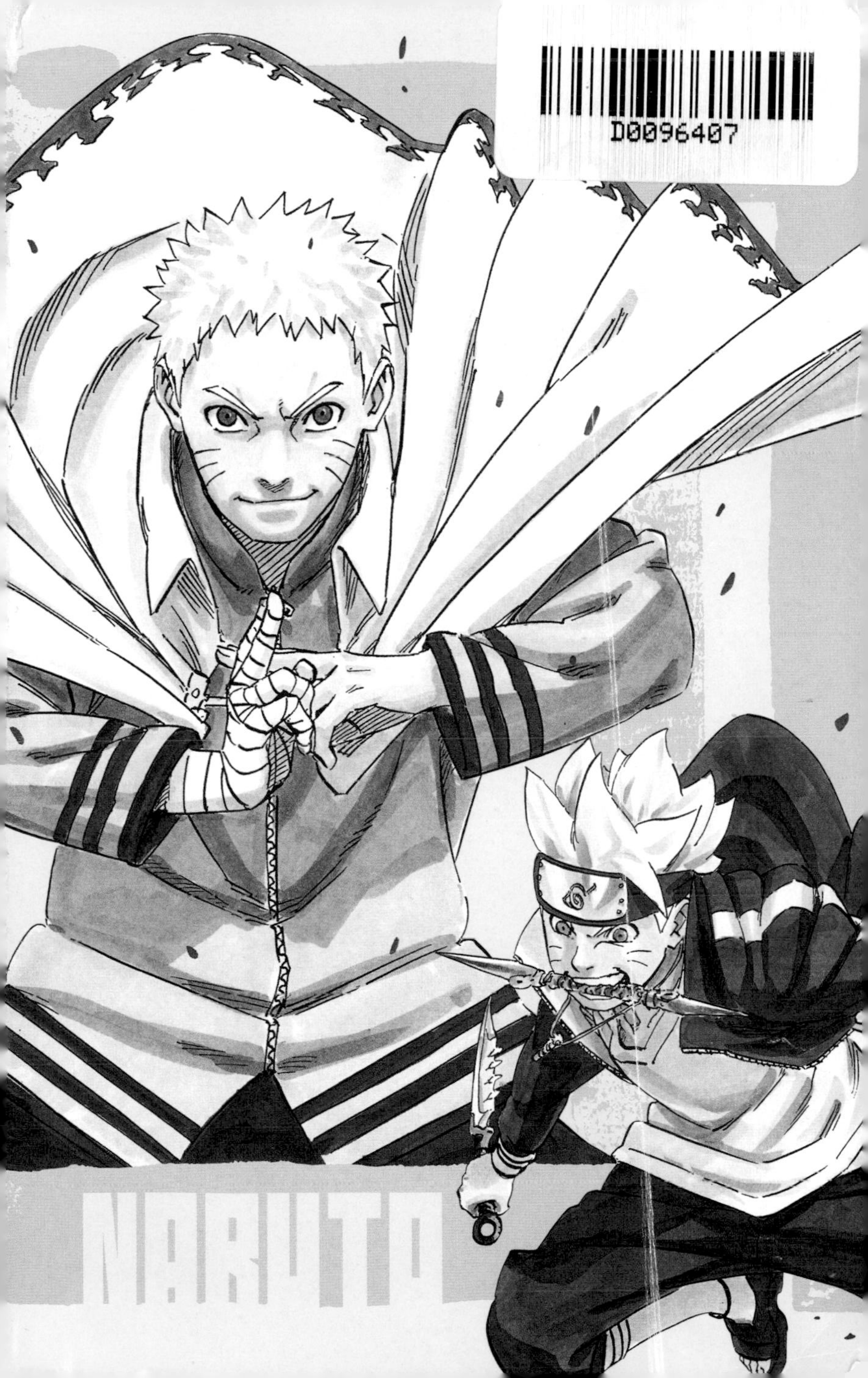
NARUTO

NARUTO'S STORY

FAMILY DAY

MASASHI KISHIMOTO

MIREI MIYAMOTO

NARUTO NARUTO-SHINDEN
© 2018 by Masashi Kishimoto, Mirei Miyamoto
All rights reserved.
First published in Japan in 2018 by SHUEISHA Inc., Tokyo.
English translation rights arranged by SHUEISHA Inc.

COVER + INTERIOR DESIGN Shawn Carrico
TRANSLATION Jocelyne Allen

Published by VIZ Media, LLC
P.O. Box 77010
San Francisco, CA 94107

Library of Congress Control Number: 2020903552

Printed in the U.S.A.
First Printing, August 2020

viz.com

shonenjump.com

CONTENTS

SHINO'S INTERLUDES

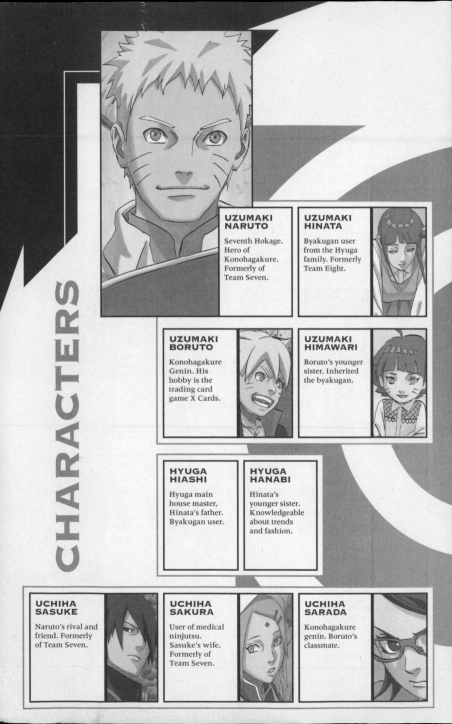

CHARACTERS

UZUMAKI NARUTO

Seventh Hokage. Hero of Konohagakure. Formerly of Team Seven.

UZUMAKI HINATA

Byakugan user from the Hyuga family. Formerly Team Eight.

UZUMAKI BORUTO

Konohagakure Genin. His hobby is the trading card game X Cards.

UZUMAKI HIMAWARI

Boruto's younger sister. Inherited the byakugan.

HYUGA HIASHI

Hyuga main house master, Hinata's father. Byakugan user.

HYUGA HANABI

Hinata's younger sister. Knowledgeable about trends and fashion.

UCHIHA SASUKE

Naruto's rival and friend. Formerly of Team Seven.

UCHIHA SAKURA

User of medical ninjutsu. Sasuke's wife. Formerly of Team Seven.

UCHIHA SARADA

Konohagakure genin. Boruto's classmate.

AKIMICHI CHOJI

Baika expansion jutsu user. Formerly of Team Ten, part of the Ino-Shika-Cho formation.

AKIMICHI KARUI

Choji's wife. Formerly a Kumogakure ninja.

AKIMICHI CHO-CHO

Konohagakure genin. Loves to eat.

NARA SHIKAMARU

Hokage advisor, Formerly of Team Ten, part of the Ino-Shika-Cho formation.

NARA TEMARI

Fifth Kazekage. Gaara's older sister. Shikamaru's wife.

NARA SHIKADAI

Konohagakure genin. Boruto's close friend.

YAMANAKA SAI

Cartoon Beast Mimicry user. Former Anbu Black Ops.

YAMANAKA INO

Family runs Yamanaka Flowers. Formerly of Team Ten, part of the Ino-Shika-Cho formation.

YAMANAKA INOJIN

Son of Sai and Ino. Inherited Cartoon Beast Mimicry.

ROCK LEE

Konohagakure's hardworking genius. Formerly of Team Three.

METAL LEE

Rock's son. Hard worker, but weak when it's time to perform.

TENTEN

Owner of the ninja hardware shop Ningu Tententen. Formerly of Team Three.

HATAKE KAKASHI

Sixth Hokage. Master of Naruto's Team Seven.

INUZUKA KIBA

Ninja dog user, partnered with Akamaru. Formerly of Team Eight.

ABURAME SHINO

Ninja Academy teacher. Formerly of Team Eight.

PROLOGUE

"Family Day?" asked Uzumaki Naruto, the Seventh Hokage. His voice echoed in his office, which was cluttered with scrolls and half-sealed cardboard boxes. He tossed the document he was reading onto his desk and lifted his face to turn a bewildered gaze on Nara Shikamaru, Advisor to the Hokage.

"Mm-hmm. They want us to give the new holiday a name. The new townspeople," Shikamaru added by way of explanation, but it still didn't click for Naruto.

"A name?" he probed further. "What's that supposed to mean?"

"Dunno. Guess it's like how you give a festival a name. And those new townsfolk have a different understanding of the word holiday to begin with."

"Hmm." Naruto's reply was vague as he fixed his gaze on the door to his office, as though he could see through it to the Hokage Rock on the other side, and the new town that spread out beyond that.

@ @ @ @ @

Some years earlier, Pain's attack at the start of the Fourth Great Ninja War had turned the village of Konohagakure into an empty wasteland, nothing but crushed houses in the cratered earth. The very foundation of the village had been ripped out and sent flying. But one thing remained untouched: Hokage Rock. And Konoha was Hokage Rock. It was unthinkable to the people of the village to rebuild Konoha in a new territory, turning their backs on the generations of Hokage who had watched over them for so many years. The sentiment that they would rebuild in this place led to the village's recovery, along with other astounding developments.

The general store, in operation since the founding of the village, transformed itself into a twenty-four-hour general store that would stay open even after sunset. Steel rails were laid in and outside of the village, and a long, slender iron box called the Raisha began to run along them. Exchanges with other villages became much easier thanks to this innovation, now that a return trip no longer required several days.

Tall buildings sprang up behind Hokage Rock, and the massive monitors built into their walls showed news not just from the Land of Fire, but from every other nation as well. The elder advisors were against these abominations. They insisted it was outrageous to have buildings overlooking Hokage Rock, but there was no denying the buildings' convenience, and the complaints gradually ceased.

The apartment buildings made room for hundreds of new residents, enticing even more people to move to the village, until the population was said to be more civilian than ninja. Even the academy from which Naruto had graduated saw a drop in applications to below capacity for ninjutsu subjects and was forced to share the facility with regular classes. Those were just the times they lived in. Although perhaps this was proof that the people of the land were at peace.

No longer hidden, the village of Konohagakure was now the largest city in the Land of Fire.

@ @ @ @ @

Naruto and the other natives of the village called this string of tall buildings "the new town." Of course, that was simply for convenience; there was no qualitative difference between *new* and *old* in Konoha. Even if the majority of people in the new town were not ninja, they were all equally family to Naruto.

Of course, differences in the lifestyles between those who were ninja and those who were not often came up. One of these differences was over holidays. The ninja world was unstable and inconsistent, with no set work hours, and it was difficult to plan for a particular day off. Holidays were, there-fore, days when the ninja happened not to have any missions. Few ninja placed any special importance on days off since they never knew when they would be.

But for civilians, a holiday was a scheduled day of relax-ation. And these non-ninja requested a day off every week, along with some kind of commemorative holiday. Holidays were certainly where the conflicting lifestyles came into play.

"Well, just making the day red on the calendar's a little ineffectual and all." Naruto picked up his Hokage seal. "I guess it could have a name. Got no reason to be against, believe it." He pushed the seal onto the document in front of him.

"Then that's settled." Shikamaru immediately tossed the paper into the "approved" tray.

And so, Family Day became a holiday in the village of Konohagakure.

"But, 'Family Day,'" Naruto mused. "What does that mean exactly?"

"According to the application, it's a day to strengthen the bond between parent and child," Shikamaru told him. "Pretty hefty burden for a single day to carry. I guess it's basically for families to go out and do something together. Shopping, a trip, stuff like that."

"The bond between parent and child... Huh." A shadow fell across Naruto's face. He thought of his own children, Boruto and Himawari. When had they last spent time together, anyway?

"Maybe we ought to go spend some time that day with our kids too." Shikamaru's voice grew brighter, perhaps guessing at Naruto's thoughts. "You have to take a break at home some-times. I know you just fall into bed. You barely even say hi to your kids, yeah? I'll help make some time in your schedule."

"Heh heh, thanks!" Naruto and Shikamaru exchanged smiles and then dropped their eyes to the floor. The pile of documents spilling off the desk and scattered onto the floor could easily be mistaken for a pattern on the ground at this point. "We'll make the time, yeah?"

"Yeah." But Shikamaru's voice sounded the slightly hopeless.

"Family Day," Naruto replied, weakly. "It'll work out. I'm definitely gonna go home. Believe it!"

1
FATHER AND DAUGHTER, RACING THROUGH KONOHA

He didn't go home. Or more precisely, he was heading home for Family Day, but it was early morning, the sun still rising up into the sky. He'd have to sleep through until evening once he made it to the house, and the whole day would be wasted.

Naruto staggered through the deserted residential area, feeling almost drunk. But he hadn't been drinking; he was just utterly and overwhelmingly exhausted.

"Hah…aaah." A large yawn spilled out of his mouth, and tears welled up at the corner of his eyes. How many days had it been since he'd slept? He'd been working so hard lately that the answer was hazy. Simply going over all those documents was a lot of work; once merchants had found out about the establishment of Family Day, they'd flooded into the Hokage's office with requests to set up stalls and kiosks. Spots had to be secured, security assigned. He'd only finished up an hour earlier.

As Naruto was getting ready to head out at last, Shizune, unable to just stand by and see him in that condition, had offered Naruto a pill to help him stay awake. But the pill smelled like a dirty fish tank, so he'd politely declined. Thinking about it now, however, maybe he should've simply accepted it instead of being so fussy.

Somnolence was serious business. The piles of garbage bags on the sides of the road looked cozily comfortable, perfect for a nap, and Naruto was excessively jealous of a cat he spotted sleeping on top of a wall, looking too content.

According to his master, Jiraiya, anything related to the "three desires"—alcohol, money, women—ruined a ninja. So even if he succumbed to this overpowering desire for sleep, he would still be a respectable ninja. It would be entirely within his rights as a ninja to clap his hands in front of the snoozing cat, startle it into wakefulness, and then gloat, "Gotcha!" The lack of maturity of such an act, however, was another issue entirely.

As he silently apologized to the cat, his house finally came into view, looking like a two-layer cake with a bucket on top. Some said it was too modest a residence for the Hokage given that he governed the entire village, but if they'd built some luxurious mansion that screamed extravagance, his dearly departed master would have taken him to task for "drowning in a lust for money." And that sort of house wasn't what Naruto actually wanted, anyway.

"I'm home," he said as he opened the door to the house quietly so as not to wake his wife and children, who were likely still asleep. (And he didn't have the energy to produce anything louder anyway.)

However, his utterance of "home" was louder than he'd intended. Or somehow his intended greeting turned into something more like a question—"I'm hooome?"

"Himawari?" For some reason, his daughter, Himawari, was sleeping in the entryway. "Hima? Hey, you okay?"

She was wrapped tightly in a blanket, so he didn't think she'd collapsed there because she was sick, but… He shook her shoulder and her small eyelids lifted slightly.

"Oh, Daddy. You're home."

"What're you doing sleeping here?"

Himawari, bleary-eyed from waking up, and Naruto, bleary-eyed from lack of sleep, looked at each other. The answer to both of their questions seemed to be that they were both equally drowsy.

"Hmm?" Himawari rubbed her eyes, still lost in sleep. A crumpling sound came from her clutched fist. "Oh!" she said, a sharp light growing in her eyes. "Daddy, here! Buy this!"

A hand extended out from beneath the blanket as she unfolded the ball of paper—a flyer—and pushed it toward him.

"Nine Tails…Kuraa-ma…" Naruto read the enormous round text out loud. In addition to the words, the flyer also featured a photograph of a long, slender egg alongside a cutified illustration of fox with an abundance of fluffy tails.

A fox with many tails given the name Kuraa-ma…

His mind started to ask the question, but there was something more important at that moment. He looked down at the blanket pooling onto the step into the house. "Did you maybe…wait here just so you could show me this?"

"Uh-huh." Himawari nodded. "When she went out yesterday, Mommy said you would be home soon."

"Unh…" The innocent words were a hook digging into his heart. It was true, he had told his wife, Hinata, that he'd try to finish up with work and come home the day before so that they could enjoy a leisurely Family Day together.

"Sorry. I had all this work… It just never ended." He ran a hand over his closely cropped hair as he made his excuses. And then he frowned. "Did your mom go out?" He peered into the house above Himawari's head. Second floor, bedroom, living room... He couldn't sense Hinata anywhere.

"Uh-huh. Yesterday morning. She said she was going to Grandpa's."

Two people fell into the category of Himawari's grandfather. Naruto's father, Minato, had passed on over thirty years earlier, so the grandpa that Hinata had gone to see was Hyuga Hiashi.

"She went to Grandpa's? What, again?"

Hiashi was the head of the Hyuga family. Had she been planning to pop by and see him? Yesterday morning was a whole day ago. She hadn't said anything about being out of the house for so long.

Actually, it had been none other than Naruto himself saying he would be home last night. Hinata had merely taken him at his word, which was exactly why she had decided to leave the kids to him. In other words, he had betrayed his wife's trust.

Aah, I really stepped in it. Naruto slumped down in the entryway, head hanging.

"Daddy, are you okay? Why are you like Mr. Turtle now?"

"Oh... It's nothing. Really..." He staggered to his feet and waved a hand. "Are *you* okay, Himawari? Mom's been gone since yesterday morning, yeah? What'd you do for food?"

"Mommy made breakfast and lunch for me. There was no supper, though." Himawari glanced over her shoulder at the second floor. "So Boruto made supper for me."

"He did?" Following Himawari's gaze, Naruto also turned his eyes toward Boruto's room. He could hear a faint snoring.

That kid... He's really got the big brother thing together, huh?

"Heh heh. That right? Boruto cooked?" Naruto rubbed the bottom of his nose, trying to hide the grin spreading across his face. "What'd he make?"

"Ummm." Himawari hung her head and thought hard for a minute. "A fried egg thing and a fried meat thing! Oh, and rice!"

"Yeah?" Although she responded not with the name of the dish but the ingredients, he still managed to get the basic idea. The important thing was that Boruto was watching out for his little sister. So it was all good. Probably.

Now that he was thinking about it, Naruto could smell something kind of burnt wafting over from the kitchen. He imagined the blackened frying pan and the dirty dishes filling the sink. "Well then, your dad here'll figure something out for supper today. For now, though, let me sleep a bit." An inadvertent yawn spilled out of his mouth. "You're still tired, too, right, Himawari? You gotta get a real sleep in your futon, not out on this hard floor. Woh-kay! How about I carry you to your room?" He moved to wrap his arms around his daughter.

"No!" She pushed him back, fierce in her rejection.

"Huh?" Her unexpected reaction threw him for a serious loop.

"You can't sleep!" Himawari brandished the flyer again. The *Nine Tails! Kuraa-ma!* flyer. "Let's go buy this right now, okay?"

"Uh. Oh." Naruto was reassured that that was all it was. "Got it. But later. I'm totally wiped right now."

"Later's no good! Look! See here?" Himawari pointed to a part of the flyer: "Special sale! Family Day only!" A campaign to take advantage of the holiday. Had one of the merchants filling his office come up with this? The sly ways they sniffed out every opportunity to make a sale would make even a ninja user of ocular jutsu click their tongue for shame. "See? We can't buy it except for today!"

"There's nothing you can only buy today. If you just hang on until your next birthday, I'll get ya a couple toys like that. Or ka-wham! A whole mountain of 'em. Believe it."

"Noooo!" Himawari, rejected again, let loose a scream that echoed piercingly in his sleep-deprived head.

He winced. "It's just Daddy is…"

The hand brandishing the flyer started to drop slowly, and his daughter's eyes were sharp as she glared up at him. "You never keep your promises."

"Hngh!" The words were a straight punch right in the gut. He desperately wanted to deny it, but sadly, Himawari was right. He'd promised to take her out more than once, but then when he still had work left on his plate, he'd sent a shadow doppelganger for her. And then the jutsu had come undone and he'd been found out.

"Tr-trust your dad," he said anyway. "I'll definitely take you out to play later. Okay?"

Himawari puffed her cheeks up, sulking, and said nothing in reply.

"Ha ha… Ha." Naruto stepped out of the entryway with a hoarse laugh and moved toward his own room. One step, two steps, Himawari's eyes boring into his back the whole time. His steps gradually grew smaller until Naruto stopped at five. He set his hands on his hips and took a deep breath, face toward the ground.

"Hah!" He slapped his cheeks as hard as he could.

"D-Daddy?"

He turned back toward a surprised Himawari and gave a big, winning smile. "I'm just gonna go take a quick shower. You go and get ready, too, okay?"

Himawari blinked rapidly. "Okay!" She quickly smiled and ran off to her own room upstairs.

After hearing the door close, Naruto slapped his cheeks again, this time even harder than before.

"What the…"

Standing in front of Masuda Toys, the toy store in the old part of town, Naruto was speechless. Masuda couldn't begin to compare with the larger retailer in the new town in terms of square footage or variety of merchandise. But unlike the larger store, which ordered in toys indiscriminately, Masuda maintained an assortment of goods that never failed to be exactly what children were looking for. If it was the latest video game that was suddenly all the rage, they would throttle back orders when the children started to lose interest. Or else they'd pivot and focus their sales on some character merchandise everyone else expected to flop, and so they were occasionally the origin of new trends.

Masuda was Naruto's preferred purveyor of toys. Not so much because of their sales savvy and curated lineup, but because—more than anything else—it was close to the house. Every time he passed by, he would remember Himawari's excitement about the toys or little Boruto's joy at getting any present at all, and his heart would grow warmer.

And now Masuda was blocked from sight by a throng of people, all of them pressed up against the store as though they were protesting it for some reason. The majority gathered were housewives Naruto's age and a little older. Strained voices rose up from the crowd.

"Hey! Hurry up and open already!"

"How long you planning on making us wait?! What're you going to do if our legs turn to stone standing out here?! Our legs turn to stone, and we're basically stone puppets, yeah? Are you saying you want to use us for shuriken practice?!"

"You know what we call this? A daimyo shop! Da! I! Myo! Getting too big for your britches, huh, Masuda?!"

Incidentally, it was still early morning, before the store's usual business hours.

Naruto watched from a distance as he turned to Himawari next to him, her eyes similarly wide. "It can't be that everyone here—they all came because of that flyer?"

"Prob'ly, Yeah. Kuraa-ma's super popular right now."

"Huh," was all Naruto could say in response, overwhelmed by the fiery heat of the housewives.

"L-ladies! Please calm down!" The plaintive plea reached his ears, clear even in the sea of angry cries. It was the Masuda shop clerk. She stood in front of the shutters, cowering like a rabbit surrounded by a pack of lions. "The store will be opening soon! To avoid crowding inside, please enter the shop one at a time! I'll ask you to form a queue now, so the person at the front—"

"A queue? You've *got* to be kidding me!"

"That's right! Can you definitively say who was first or second?"

"N-no… That's…" The clerk cowered further.

"Yeah! Are you going to make things right if some idiot who came along later lines up ahead of me?!"

"In that case, I'll distribute numbers via a lottery," the clerk suggested. "So the person who gets the first—"

"A lottery! Ha! Don't give us that! My kid's at home, dying to have this thing! Now hurry up and open the store!"

"Right! Open it!" came the voices in agreement. Their children had apparently begged them for a Kuraa-ma, and so they had all been waiting in front of the shop since daybreak.

I guess this is what they mean when they say mothers are strong, he thought, pained—or rather, filled with trepidation. He had a vision of the shop clerk being crushed before his eyes by the throng of mothers. *So buying the Kuraa-ma means slipping past this scary group of moms to get inside the store?*

What if it was Hinata there instead of him there? Would she shrink before this herd of mothers? The answer came to him right away. Although she was generally a gentle woman, at her core, Hinata was a rock. He had no doubt that she would simply charge in there without a second thought if it was for the sake of their daughter.

"I didn't think it would be so popular, this Kuraa-ma thing. What kind of toy is it exactly?" he asked.

"Umm." Himawari gave him an innocent smile. "You raise this fox, a Nine Tails fox spirit."

"And the fox's name is Kuraa-ma?"

"Yeah. It's super cute, but I heard the real one isn't that cute. Like, his eyes are all buggy."

"Hmm." Naruto considered this for a moment. "Yeah, that's true maybe. He does have weird eyes."

"Daddy, you saw the real Kuraa-ma?" Her eyes opened wide in awe.

"Just for a sec." It seemed that this Kuraa-ma was indeed *Kurama*. He was pretty sure he remembered seeing a document asking for the right to develop merchandise patterned after Nine Tails. Kurama—once feared as a catastrophic force, the creature that scarred the village deeply—was now a product, a commodity for people to purchase. A small thorn that had pierced Naruto's heart abruptly dropped away. The hatred and fear that had been directed at Kurama faded, and he felt like he could finally accept the spirit. He had pressed his seal onto this deeply resonant document, but he never dreamed they would turn the fox into a toy for children...

At any rate, it seemed his judgement had been correct. Naruto considered the situation carefully while he watched his daughter chatter happily.

"So, at first, it's in an egg, and you pet it and tap it and cheer it on, and then it comes out of the egg."

"Are foxes born from eggs?" He felt like that wasn't right, but then he wondered. A question mark floated above his head.

"It's all round and happy if you give it little food pellets to eat. They're called 'hyorogan,' and there are a bunch of kinds. If you feed it a red one, then its fur gets darker."

"This Kuraa-ma sure eats adorable things, huh?"

"If you bop it on the head, you can play together," she noted.

"So you bop it on the head, this Kuraa-ma." He imagined his daughter giving the adorable fox from the flyer a hard pop. It was a fairly startling image, but he guessed kids wouldn't be hitting it so fiercely as all that. Even still, a wry smile crossed his face. "So it's born from an egg, you get food for it. Dunno. Sounds almost like a baby, this Kuraa-ma."

Himawari simply blinked several times, perhaps not really understanding what he was saying.

Just when Naruto's grin was fading, he heard a voice that echoed from the depths of his stomach. *"Hey. Just who are you calling a baby?"*

Kuraa-ma—or rather the genuine article, the real Kurama. He sounded extremely dissatisfied, as if he had never expected to be treated like a baby and didn't actually much care for it, even if it was just a fictional character based on the real him.

It would be a hassle later on if that sentiment took root. Naruto turned his mind inward to reply, but then one of the Masuda customers suddenly called out to him, and he missed his chance to talk with Kurama.

"Oh? Just when I was wondering who it was in the back there, if it isn't Naruto!"

"Kiba! Weird to see you here."

The voice belonged to a classmate from his academy days, a war buddy who'd stood with him on the line between life and death any number of times before: Inuzuka Kiba. The hair that stuck out every which way when they were kids was now pulled back neatly, giving him a rough look in line with his tapered jaw.

Something white moved sluggishly at his feet: the ninja dog Akamaru. He made his way over to Naruto, as if trying to escape from the crowd of clamoring mothers, and then promptly laid down. He was getting close to being a very old dog, and all the commotion was probably annoying.

And then a puppy came trotting over from behind: Akemaru, looking very much like Akamaru when he was small.

"You want to talk weird, I could say the same for you here with your daughter all proper. 'Sup. You out shopping with your dad today?"

Himawari was reaching out to pet Akemaru, but when Kiba spoke to her, she nodded and hid behind Naruto.

"Come on. It's not nice not to say hello." Naruto tried to make her apologize for her rudeness, but Kiba didn't seem to mind at all.

"Nah, nah, it's fine. Being shy like that, maybe a little scared of new people, she takes after Hinata. But, like, she's gotten a lot bigger, huh? She was just this big the other day." He brought his hands up in front of his chest to indicate a space of about a foot.

"Okay, look, she was never that small," Naruto said. "She's not a puppy."

"You got no idea, all right? Especially when you see her every day." Kiba laughed cheerfully and then continued.

"Anyway, we're here. Yours got her eyes on that Kuraa-ma, too?"

"Yeah. Himawari begged me." He stroked the hair of the girl still hiding behind him. "And what about you? Don't tell me—you got sick of the dogs, so you're trading them in for a fox, yeah?"

"Heh! You gotta be kidding. A friend just asked me to, so..." Kiba trailed off. "Aah, she didn't actually ask me. It's just she saw the flyer and got all carried away by how cute the fox is, so I figured...maybe I could surprise her with one..." His eyes darted about, his voice sinking away into nothing.

Naruto watched him with surprise.

"What's that look about?!" Kiba demanded.

"It's just, it's a surprise for your girlfriend, yeah?" he said. "That's great, though! With you and Shino both single, Hinata worries."

"Th-this has got nothing to do with the old Team Eight!"

"Huh. So you got a fox-loving girlfriend." Naruto smirked.

"Let me tell you right now!" the other man protested. "She's a real hard-core cat lover. Although with cats, I guess it'd be more soft-core? Anyway, she's a devoted woman! She just got a little tiny bit tricked by a fox, that's all!" He was getting too worked up over nothing, and he quickly regained his composure. "But, well, running into you here, I guess our timing's not the greatest."

"What do you mean?"

"Kuraa-ma." Kiba jerked his thumb over his shoulder toward Masuda. "I looked into it a bit. Kuraa-ma's way too popular. And they're getting ten today at best, maybe twenty if they're lucky."

"Wha—That's all?!" Naruto guessed there were nearly a hundred people pressed up in front of the shop, meaning only one in ten or so would be able to get a Kuraa-ma.

"I don't want to compete with your kid. But, well, no hard feelings, you know, if only one of us manages to get—"

The shutters over Masuda's door slowly began to rise, cutting Kiba off. Naruto could see what were likely the manager's fingers in the gap above the ground, and then the shutters were all the way up. Opening time.

The earth shook as everyone in front of the shop surged inside as a single being.

"Ah?! Crap. They're all getting in before me!" Kiba hurriedly pushed his way through the crowd, leaving his beloved dogs behind as he melted into the human tsunami.

Jeers and angry cries echoed from inside the small store, and Naruto even heard screaming as people got stepped on. It was all-out war in there. He swallowed hard and looked down at Himawari for a final check.

"What d'you think? You gonna wait here?"

Himawari looked up at him. Her expression had been anxious upon hearing about the low stock, but she was apparently not ready to give up. She shook her head from side to side.

"Woh-kay!" Naruto steeled himself as he took her hand, stepped over the sleeping Akamaru, and went after Kiba.

He proceeded past the various doodads crammed together, knocked about by the chaos of customers. Unable to take a real breath in the stuffy room, he was very likely to lose Himawari's hand if he dropped his guard for even an instant.

"Sorry! Couldja let me through here?" He headed further into the store, carving out a path between people with his shoulders. He had no idea where the Kuraa-ma would be in the midst of all this confusion, but he guessed they would probably be near the cash register.

Several of the customers noticed Naruto and cried out.

"Lord Hokage!"

"Lord Seventh?!"

He had no time to respond, however, and merely cut through them with a knife hand instead of bowing in greeting. "Coming through... Ow! ...Oh! You just hit me with an elbow! Don't worry about it...Hm? You waited all night? What a coincidence. I was up all night, too. I was!"

For some reason, more than one person in the crowd complained to him about the chaos, and he answered each of them rather noncommittally. When he finally managed to reach the cash register, there was a sign that read "Family Day only! Limited time special!" just as he'd expected.

There it is!

He grabbed a long, slender egg, quickly bought it, and then slid away from the register area, going against the tide of people. When Naruto once again crossed the threshold to the outside world, Akamaru wagged his tail in greeting, as if to congratulate him on a job well done.

Naruto finally took a deep breath while the joy of victory coursed through his veins. "Yesssss!" He held the bag in his hand high in the air. "A ton of people in there, but we managed to get this thing!"

He exchanged a grin with Himawari, who was clinging to his back. Her hair was a mess, likely because of that vortex of chaos they'd passed through together, and beads of sweat popped up on her forehead.

Kiba came out of Masuda while Naruto was tidying Himawari's hair, his shoulders slumped in disappointment. "Dammit... They're sold out..." Other dejected customers followed him out and trudged away.

"You didn't get one?" Naruto raised an eyebrow. "But you got in there before we did."

"I didn't know where they were." Kiba shrugged. "And with so many people in there, my nose wasn't any help. Dang."

"Aah, well, you can't use your nose to look for toys, anyway." Naruto rolled his eyes.

"Daddy?" Himawari tugged on his sleeve. She was staring at the bag with the egg in it anxiously.

A wry smile on his face, he handed her the bag. Beaten down by a human tsunami after several all-nighters in a row, every muscle in his body was crying out in exhaustion. But it was all worth it if he got to see his daughter's happy face.

However.

"Ah." The look on her face as she pulled the egg from the bag was not what he'd been expecting.

Kiba peered at her hand and furrowed his brow. "Hey, um, Naruto?"

"Hm?" Naruto also dropped his gaze. And then doubted his eyes. "'One Tail! Shukaa-ku'?" Instead of the adorable fox with its many bushy tails, there was a portly, plump tanuki with a round tail drawn on the egg. "It's not Kuraa-ma?!"

"That's... It's a copycat product made in Sunagakure, y'know? You raise a One Tail instead of Nine Tails," Kiba explained, but Naruto wasn't listening. He hurried back into the store and ran down the aisle, an easy feat now that most of the customers had departed.

Stunned, he stared at the cash register. The sign hanging there was the "Family Day only! Limited time special!" that Naruto had seen. But below it, beside a basket that said "Smash hit! Nine Tails! Kuraa-ma!" was another basket that suggested, "How about a tanuki, too?" Two baskets. The Shukaa-ku eggs were still piled high, clearly not the most popular item of the day.

"Uh...mm," Naruto said to the clerk at the register, turning his eyes toward the Kuraa-ma basket, which didn't have so much as a mote of dust in it. "So I guess...you don't have any Kuraa-ma?"

The clerk shook her head, a profoundly apologetic look on her face.

He made his way back outside on weak legs, and Himawari burst into tears. Her small shoulders shook hard, and the two ninja dogs paced anxiously around her.

"Okay, listen. Once the fad is over, it'll be a piece of cake to get a toy like that!" Kiba nervously tried to comfort Naruto's daughter. "Your birthday's still a ways off, yeah? By then, you'll be able to get one of those foxes so easy it'll make this whole thing now a joke. Aah, for real. Absolutely!"

"Kiba."

"And your dad's the Hokage, yeah? That's such a huge deal that even someone like *me* couldn't be Hokage. Your dad goes and talks to someone, and any toy you want'll be—"

"Kiba," Naruto interrupted. "That's enough. Believe it."

"You say that. But you…" Kiba looked from the sobbing Himawari to Naruto and back again. His meaning was crystal clear: *What're you going to do about this kid now?*

"Himawari," Naruto murmured as he put a hand on her shaking shoulders. "Sorry. I should've double-checked. I was just in a panic."

The small hands that had been wiping tears away stopped suddenly to reveal eyes that were swollen and bright red from crying. Naruto didn't look away, but instead carefully held her gaze.

"I'll get one."

"What?" Himawari asked in reply.

"A Kuraa-ma," he said. "And I'm not talking about next time here. No way. I'll get one today. Believe it."

She hung her head for a moment, but finally nodded and rubbed her eyes before flashing him a shy smile. Naruto figured that was enough. Just so long as she wasn't crying.

"What d'you wanna do? You're not actually going to exercise your Hokage privileges, are you?"

Naruto laughed off Kiba's question. "I don't have any privileges that are that convenient. They started sales on Family Day, so that must mean they ramped production just for today. I'll just use my shadow doppelgangers to go around to every single store."

"Shadow doppelgangers, huh?" Kiba snorted. "You stink like you're exhausted after a mission. You still got enough in you for doppelgangers?"

"I'm just sleep deprived is all. Art of Multiple Shadow Clones!" White smoke puffed up around them as Naruto wove the signs to produce...two clones. Several hundredths of what he usually managed. He froze, fingers still crossed, and broke into a cold sweat.

"There's just two of 'em. You said 'multiple.' You're making me roll my eyes over here." Kiba flicked each doppelganger on the forehead. There was a shredding sound, and then they vanished.

"Ah?!" Naruto cried.

"Idiot. Doppelgangers aren't gonna do you any good. Today's basically a festival. All that's gonna happen is they'll get knocked around by the crowd and disappear. That's it," Kiba asserted. "How 'bout I give you a hand? My nose doesn't work in the shops, either, but I can pick up on the Kuraa-ma. I just need to find the scent trail of the red earth and dandelions used in the ink, and it'll all be good."

When he saw that Naruto was baffled by the sudden proposal, Kiba said, "Don't get the wrong idea. I don't care either way if your stock goes down, but I'm not gonna sleep too good after the girl cried on us like that. I know I said 'no hard feelings' before, but...it's like...when she's crying like that, it's a little..." He scratched his cheek awkwardly. "Listen. I'll go look in the new town. You take the old town. If you find Ku-raa-ma first, then get into Sage Mode and come—Oh, in your condition, that's prob'ly a no-go. Well, I'll come join you when I feel like it. Don't go anywhere with extra weird smells."

"Okay." Naruto nodded.

"Awright. C'mon, guys!" Kiba headed toward Hokage Rock, Akamaru and Akemaru trailing behind him.

Naruto watched until he disappeared into the thronging crowd and then crouched down, back turned toward Hi-mawari. "Woh-kay. Should we get going, too?"

"Yeah!" She scrambled eagerly onto his back.

It was just like Kiba said: kids grew up way faster than their parents realized. He was sure she'd been lighter the last time he'd given her a piggyback—another thing you don't notice when you see each other every day. But did Kiba's words really apply to Naruto now? Lately, he barely saw Himawari every other day.

No.

He had to do what he could for her now, not just look back on the past. With resolve in his heart, Naruto started to run.

◎　◎　◎　◎　◎

"You got any Nine Tails? Kuraa-ma?!" Naruto yelled as he flew into the first place he saw, the twenty-four-hour general store.

The sales clerk gaped at the sudden appearance of the Seventh Hokage.

"Oh! Daddy, over there! There's lots of them!"

"Really?!" He turned his eyes to a shelf by the cash register. And indeed, he saw eggs that looked like the real thing on display. "They're all Shukaa-ku, huh?"

"They are." The clerk nodded.

As far as he could see, each and every one of them was a ta-nuki. He actually felt a little bad for the toy, which was clearly not selling at all. And why were so many Sunagakure toys being sold in Konohagakure to begin with? He was starting to suspect that the things hadn't sold at all in the other village and now were being passed along to his town.

"Might be funny to buy a bunch and send 'em to Gaara," he mused.

"Gaara?" his daughter asked.

"A friend in Sunagakure. When we were kids, he was aaaalways with Shukaku—I mean, Shukaa-ku. When he and Shukaa-ku got separated, it was a whole thing in and of itself."

"Was he lonely after the tanuki was gone?" Himawari wondered. "He must have really loved it."

"Nah, not quite. Woh-kay! Next store!" With the same force that he had entered the shop with, Naruto dashed out of the general store.

◎ ◎ ◎ ◎ ◎

"Kuraa-ma? That toy that's all the rage lately? Nope, don't have it. Actually, let me ask you, did you really think we'd have it? As you can well see, this is a flower shop."

He'd gone into Yamanaka Flowers along the way because he had nothing to lose by giving it a try. The shop was run by Yamanaka Ino, one of his classmates from the academy, and while flowers of all hues and colors greeted them, there was not a single toy in sight.

"Yeah, I guess not." Naruto sighed. "What's Sai up to, any-way?"

"He's out with Inojin. I can give him a message if you needed something."

"Nah, it's nothing like that. Sorry to bug you at work." Naruto waved a hand.

"It's fine. Oh, Naruto! Wait! Hang on!" Ino stopped him and pulled out one of the many flowers lining the walls. "Here, for you, Himawari." She handed Himawari a sunflower—a *himawari*—in full bloom.

"Wow! Thanks, Auntie!" she responded joyfully. She'd been shy with Kiba, but perhaps the gift of a flower bearing her own name helped her to let her guard down now.

"Ooh, calling me 'Auntie'! Maybe I'll just give you one more as a bonus!" And another sunflower did indeed join its companion in Himawari's hand.

The girl was even more thrilled, and she waved enthusiastically as Ino saw them off.

"I know you just got them and all, but you can't hang onto your old dad if you've got those flowers in your hands. How about we drop by the house first and leave them there?" Naruto suggested.

"Whaaat? No! I'll carry them! If I poke 'em in here, they won't be in the way." The "here" that she selected was the collar of his shirt. *Skrtch, skrtch*. He felt the stems rub against his back.

"Oh, yeah?" He turned his gaze toward the show window next to them and saw his own self reflected back, sunflowers sticking up off his head like antennas. Quite the lively fashion. "You think they suit me?" he asked Himawari.

She laughed in return. "They're perfect!"

"Heh heh heh heh!" Naruto laughed, slightly embarrassed.

"The wee ones these days… It's all beep boop beep boop. They're obsessed with their beep booping. Don't have the time of day for the old games," the old lady groaned, a difficult look on her face. She'd been running the ancient sweet shop for too long to remember, wrinkled since Naruto was a kid, and that hadn't changed now; she was still covered in wrinkles.

Entranced by the candies, Himawari cocked her head to one side, lips covered with kinako sweet powder. "What's a beep boop?"

"Boruto plays with one during supper," Naruto said. "A beep boop. That's what she's talking about. Believe it."

"That's not a beep boop," the old lady argued. "That's the star of hope for the next generation of toys, the light-en-ing scroll."

"It's different? So then, what's a beep boop?"

"A beep beep's a beep boop. You get a title and put on these airs, but you can't even tell a beep boop from a lightning scroll. That's a sad state," the old woman grumbled as she pulled a package off a shelf. "Now then. I s'pose you're looking for that Kuraa-ma or whatever it is."

"You got any?!" Naruto's heart thumped hard in his chest.

"Nope. Unfortunately, there are none here. None of that… but I got something even better." The old lady assumed an air of importance and then pulled out the contents of the package. "Origami."

He was speechless.

"What's that look for? This is muuuuch more fun than any beep boop or what have you."

"Himawari." He turned to his daughter. "Let's get your mouth cleaned up there."

"Mm." She nodded.

"Aah!" the woman cried. "Leave it! Quit that! Don't use

that to wipe the wee one's mouth! It's not a napkin, you know! Now listen! Get folding! Hurry up and fold!"

"We're actually in a hurry... Well, I guess it can't hurt." He folded the paper, getting instruction from the old lady as he went. Maybe because it was the first time he'd done origami in a while, he managed to have a decent amount of fun. And Himawari also seemed pleased with the shuriken he made out of silver paper, so he strung it onto a hemp cord and hung it from her neck.

He never did find out what a beep boop was.

Naruto turned half an eye into the ninja tool shop, Ninja Tools Tententen. The owner, Tenten, was leaning back in her chair, arms hanging—she was extremely lazy.

"Caaan't sell a daaaang thing. And after I went and got some family-type kunai in stock just for the holiday. Haven't sold a siiiiingle one."

"What exactly are family-type kunai, anyway?" Naruto asked.

"Hm!" Tenten waved a hand in the general direction of the showcase, still half-lying down.

Tucked away inside were uniquely shaped kunai, each with a different blade at the end of its hilt. One was long and slender, while the other had a roundness to it like a pen nib and although short, glittered sharply at the tip.

"How's that got anything to do with family?" He raised a doubtful eyebrow.

"The long blade's the parent, and the short one's the kid," she explained. "See? Looks like a parent with their child, right?"

"Bit of stretch, don't you think?" Naruto commented. "Anyway, you got this toy, Nine Tails Kuraa-ma?"

Tenten's swaying stopped abruptly. "That's the fourth time I've gotten that question today. So is *that* what's going on? You all telling me this tool shop's behind the times? That I should close up and open a toy store already? You think so, too, Lord Seventh? That's why you asked, isn't it? The shop's a loser, so I better get a side hustle going with toys? Is that what you're trying to tell me?!"

"I don't think that, and I'm not saying that. Believe it," Naruto denied the charge weakly.

"It's true, this place isn't popular. At. All. The neighborhood kids just use the place for their little games of chicken. They say I got a huge gourd in here that speaks in a human voice. Plus, I'm way overstocked on ironware, so people come and complain that the magnetic field's wonky around here. If I could just sell wholesale to the police or the academy, I'da sold all this stuff ages ago. But noooo, they all take those contracts somewhere else…"

"Daddy, why's that lady crying?" Himawari asked.

"Hmm." Naruto paused. "I guess 'cause we're at peace maybe."

"But that's a good thing, right?"

"Sure is." Naruto decided to buy some earrings that caught his eye. Miniature kunai dangled from the ends of the clips, just big enough to sit on his fingertip.

By the time he was paying for them, Tenten was back to her old self, customer-service smile plastered on her face. "What about picking these up at the same time?" She pointed again to the family-type kunai. Naruto burst out laughing at the power of her mercenary spirit and the speed at which she switched gears.

Together with Himawari, he ran around to each and every store in the old town, but they didn't encounter a single Kuraa-ma egg. And now the sun was sinking in the sky. Naruto gritted his teeth. After all, he had the *real* Kurama inside of him and yet... His only hope now was Kiba off in the new town.

"Heyyy! Narutooooo!"

He heard Kiba's voice from above and looked up to see the man on the roof of the restaurant next to him.

"I found it!" Kiba shouted. "A real Kuraa-ma this time!"

"S-seriously?!" Naruto shouted back.

Kiba kicked at the sign and dropped down to the ground before turning toward Himawari and popping a thumb up. "Everywhere was sold out, but there was just one left at the shop at the train station. In the souvenir shop on the platform for long-distance trains to other villages. Unlike Konoha, the other villages are not particularly interested in Kuraa-ma."

"But are you sure?" Naruto asked, hesitantly. "You wanna give one to your fox-loving girlfriend, yeah?"

"She doesn't love foxes! She likes cats. And anyway, I didn't tell her I was going to get her one, so no harm no foul, basically." Kiba shrugged.

"Huh." Naruto smiled. "All right! Himawari!"

"Yeah! Thanks! ...Um, Uncle Dog Man." Himawari grinned, too.

"Heh! 'Sall good," Kiba flashed a smile, not at all put off by the title she gave him. "I got Akamaru to carry it, so should be here so—Oh! Speak of the devil!" He turned just as Akamaru and Akemaru appeared together from the sea of people.

"There ya go! The eagerly awaited Thunder Burger!" Kiba

thrust a hand into the paper bag, "Normally, I don't feed 'em junk food, but this burger's got no additives. My dogs just love 'em—Hey! This is a Thunder Burger bag?! What happened to Kuraa-ma?! Tch! There's even the change in here!"

"Hey, Kiba," Naruto muttered, uneasily. "Over there…"

A man in a hood was hurrying away from the scene, back through the crowd the dogs had just come out of. In his hand was a paper bag with a train symbol printed on it.

"Oi! No way!" Kiba yelped. "You're kidding me? Someone switched bags on you?! Akemaru?! Dammit. It's 'cause I haven't fed you since the morn—"

"Kiba!" Naruto took Himawari off his back and thrust her toward Kiba, along with all the things they were carrying. "Hang onto Himawari!"

"Hang onto her?!" Kiba gaped at the Hokage. "Hey!"

Naruto shot after the man in the crowd. Catching sight of this, the man abruptly quickened his pace, nimbly dancing past the throngs. This, added to the fact that he had tricked Akemaru (no matter how hungry the dog might have been), sealed it for Naruto: this guy was a ninja.

"Hey!" Naruto yelled. "Hold it right there!"

There wasn't a ninja in Konoha he didn't know, and the man had to have been aware of this. He pulled his hood tighter around his face to keep from being seen and started to run, indifferent to the people he bashed into in his haste.

"Hngh!" Naruto simply couldn't be as rough with the people of Konoha, and he felt compelled to stop and help passersby back to their feet as he gave chase. The man gradually pulled away from him.

This day…

He hadn't been able to do anything for Himawari. In the end, he'd done nothing but get her hopes up and then dash them to the ground. Kiba had been the one to get ahold of the Kuraa-ma the man ahead was making off with. Naruto had to at least get the thing back.

But not only had he not slept in who knew how long, he'd spent the day running around Konoha, meaning his stamina and chakra were both at rock bottom. Even if he tried a teleportation jutsu, it would probably get him nowhere, just like the doppelgangers that morning.

I don't want to make a huge commotion in the middle of the village, but desperate times!

"Kurama!" Naruto turned his mind inward and spoke to Nine Tails. *"Sorry, but couldja help me out here? Oi, Kurama?!"*

"I don't want to," came the somewhat petulant reply.

"W-why not?!"

"It's your fault for calling me a baby. And Shukaku? Of all things, that you would mistake me for that tanuki. And now you're talking to me in that tone?"

"No, no, I'm not trying to—I mean, I'm in a serious fix here! Himawari's..."

"All the more reason."

"What?"

"What I'm saying is, you can't rely on me. You have to work this out yourself. If you're not going to go all out for your daughter, then when will you? Idiot."

Naruto couldn't say anything to that. "Heh heh." He brought his mind back to reality. "Yeah, I guess he's got a point."

He already knew that Kurama was right. He had to get that Kuraa-ma with his own strength. It was just a battle of willpower and stamina now. He ran intently after the man as he wondered, *How far have I run anyway?*

The man slowed when he turned into a deserted alley. It seemed less like his strength was giving out and more like he was resigning himself to his fate somehow, as though he couldn't allow himself to flee any further.

"Gotchaaaa!" Naruto shouted and leaped at the man's back. He pushed him down onto the road and quickly peeled back the hood. Just as he'd expected, the man was a Konoha genin, one who Naruto had ordered to look into things in the borderlands.

Pinned to the ground, the man gritted his teeth and intently avoided Naruto's eyes. The man had never caused any trouble before. So why was he getting his hands dirty with petty theft?

"Daddy?"

Naruto heard a child's voice, and a boy tottered out from the alley.

"W-why are you out here?! It's okay. I'm okay, so just wait inside!" The man's voice was shaking. Naruto quickly understood the relationship between the pair from the agitation in the man's voice.

There didn't seem to be any need to hold him down, so he released the man on the ground. "What's going on here?"

The answer came not from the man, but from behind Naruto.

"Looks like he wanted to get a Kuraa-ma for his kid no matter what he had to do. Just like you." It was Kiba. When had he caught up? Beside him, Himawari sat across Akamaru's back.

Naruto turned back to the man before him, gaze probing him for the truth of this.

"My sincerest apologies!" The man sat up and pressed his forehead to the ground. "My son wanted one so desperately, so all I could think about was how to get it. I looked everywhere, but I couldn't find any, and then just as the sun was setting, I heard Kiba. Something just came over me..."

Sobbing, the man explained that he was always away from the village patrolling the edges of the country. And then finally, he had a day off. When he saw his son for the first time in far too long, the boy had timidly pleaded for a Nine Tails Kuraa-ma.

Naruto listened silently to the man's story. He had only wanted to make his child happy, and Naruto understood that feeling painfully well. But he had crossed a line that should never have been crossed. He had to be punished for the crime of theft, and in front of his son, of all things. Maybe he should at least send the boy away before he did anything.

While he was wrestling with this, Himawari slid down from Akamaru's back, picked up the paper bag with the Kuraa-ma in it, and handed it to the man. "Here. This is yours, right, mister? You shouldn't drop it."

"What?" A question mark popped up above the man's head.

"Himawari?" Naruto wore his own question mark.

She looked back at him with a faint smile just like her mother's, as if she had seen through to the heart of everything. "This man was just trying to bring the Kuraa-ma he bought to his son. Right, Daddy?"

Naruto understood what his daughter was getting at quickly enough. "Oh. Yeah." He understood, but... "Are you sure, though? I know you wanted one, too, Himawari. Pretty bad."

"It's okay. I have this." She pulled out the Shukaa-ku Naruto had bought by mistake. "It's a special present from you. I love it." And then she gently stroked the silver paper shuriken hanging around her neck. "You're always so busy, Daddy. You never play with me. But today, we got to spend the whole day going to all these different places. It was super fun. I have too many treasures now. I can't carry any more."

"Hima…" Naruto's face relaxed as the faint smile on her face was replaced with an innocent grin that showed her age.

"Whoa, whoa. If this little girl doesn't want it, I'm—" Kiba started to reach out, but Akamaru and Akemaru both snapped at him, and he quickly yanked the hand back. "Ouch!" Even still, he was smiling.

Naruto grew serious again, crouched down, and brought his face close to the man, who was still on his knees. "We're good on the Kuraa-ma thing," he declared, quietly. "But the way you were pushing around the people of the village, I can't actually let that slide."

"I know." He hung his head in dejection.

"As of today, you are released from your mission to investigate the borderlands," Naruto said.

He closed his eyes tightly, shaking in despair.

The Hokage placed a hand on his shoulder before continuing. "Starting tomorrow, you're on guard at the gate. I'll tell Shikamaru. It's the biggest landmark in Konoha, after Hokage Rock. So you better take good care of it. Believe it."

"Is this…a demotion then? Oh! No, please excuse me. I will carry out my duty to the utmost of my abilities."

Listening to the man's humble words, Kiba snorted with laughter. "Idiot. It means you don't gotta be away from the village anymore. Take good care of that son of yours."

"Oh!" Tears welled up in the corners of the man's eyes again. "Thank you so much!"

"So." Naruto pressed on his joints, stiff from a full day of being worked like a slave, as he slowly stood up. "Woh-kay. How about we head home?"

＠ ＠ ＠ ＠ ＠

"Borutoooooo! Supperrrrr! Daddy bought hamburgers! It's already nighttime! How long are you gonna sleeeeep?!" Himawari yelled for her older brother from the bottom of the stairs.

Boruto's sleepy voice came in response, and then there was the sound of the front door opening.

"Oh! Mommy! You're home! ...Yeah, he did come home... Huh? On my ears? Hee hee. Pretty great, huh? Daddy bought them for me. And this, too! And this. And this..."

It appeared that Hinata was home. For the first time in a long time, they would be able to have supper together as a family.

As he dozed on the sofa in the living room, Naruto turned his ears toward Himawari's excited voice. Normally, he slept away his days off, but he'd spent this one in a flurry of sorts. He hadn't been able to rest at all, but if anyone asked if he was unhappy about that, he would have smiled and said no. It was absolutely the right way to spend Family Day.

＠ ＠ ＠ ＠ ＠

"So you're home?"

Naruto's eyes flew open. He had apparently fallen asleep at some point and hadn't realized that Boruto was right beside him. The look on his face was sulky in the extreme. Guessing the reason for that, Naruto turned to face his son. "Sorry about yesterday."

"It's fine. Whatever," Boruto snorted, annoyed, hands clasped behind his head.

So then he wasn't mad that Naruto hadn't been able to

make it home. Which meant he was just in a bad mood because he spent the whole day sleeping? Or maybe... Naruto turned his mind toward the entryway. Himawari was still showing Hinata the various presents the day had brought her.

"You wanted to hang out today, too?" Naruto asked.

"Wha—?!" Boruto threw his head back in shock. "Why would I want *that*?! I was just—I just wanted to complain 'cause the hamburgers you brought back are so teeny..."

"The bag's not empty yet, though." Naruto pointed at the Thunder Burger bag on the desk.

Boruto glanced over at it and stiffened up. He flapped his mouth open and closed like a goldfish, looking for some other excuse.

And then Naruto noticed that he had something in his hand, a flyer, although it was mostly hidden behind his head, so he couldn't make out the details. The page was crumpled, just like with Himawari that morning, but Naruto could just barely make out the name of the shop: Ninja Tools Tententen.

Smiling wryly so as not to show that he'd guessed what was going on, Naruto put a hand in his pocket. "You'd probably rather have a video game, but... lightning scroll, was it? I don't really get that stuff, though." He pulled out a long, slender package and offered it to Boruto.

"What?" His son raised an eyebrow. "What's this?"

"It's a present. Believe it. I figured hamburgers alone weren't quite enough."

"Huh?" Cocking his head to one side, Boruto opened the package. A kunai with blades at both ends of the hilt glittered, brand-new. "This..." A grin began to spread across his face, but he quickly pursed his lips to maintain his sulk. He crumpled the kunai's packaging and whirled around. But as he was leaving the room, Naruto heard him whisper "Thanks," in the smallest voice.

"Yup." His own voice in reply was also small. He shot another wry grin after his complicated son before he settled back down on the sofa. There was someone else he had to speak with.

"So? Heeey? C'mon, stop grumping already. I picked Shukaku 'cause of a bit of a mix-up. Believe it. How long are you gonna pout? I'm absolutely fox over tanuki, you know. I mean, I get the kitsune fried tofu on my ramen and everything! Fox ramen, right? So...are you listening? Hey. I said, hey. Kurama? Kuraa-maaaa?"

1 MASTER SHINO! AND LUNCH!

Naruto had decided that they would have Family Day, and the atmosphere was festive in Konohagakure. Laughter rang out from every direction, and the food carts played a sizzling orchestra of frying food, accompanied by the lilting melody of flutes and the powerful rhythm of drums. A round of applause rose above it all, perhaps in appreciation of a street performer offering up a particularly fabulous trick to her audience. Everyone in the village was making much merry. Yes. Everyone. This man was no exception.

Family Day, huh?

Because of the metallic goggles on academy instructor Aburame Shino's face, it was generally hard to pick up on his expressions. But a smile clearly played on his lips now.

I wasn't sure if I should object to this ongoing tendency to slight single people when the holiday first came to my attention. But this is nice. Even a single person like me can enjoy the day.

Food stalls lined the street where Shino stood. In his right hand, he held fried squid, a sausage skewer, and a chocolate banana; in his left, a bucket of popcorn. He wasn't actually that hungry; he'd just gotten swept up by the festive mood.

"I wanna see a movie next! Movie!"

Hearing a familiar voice, Shino turned to see a student from the academy with her parents. She hadn't seen him, however, as she walked in the direction of the movie theater. She seemed to be having a great time.

He did feel a twinge of sadness at the sight, but it quickly disappeared. True, he was single, but he had a family to love nonetheless. And he wasn't talking about any sentimental nonsense like how all of the students at the academy were his family. No, his family was in his heart. His chest, to be precise.

Almost as if in response to the thought, the insects in his chest started making noise. The bugs gave Shino life while simultaneously making their nest inside his body; they were with him twenty-four hours a day, in sickness and in health, in joy and in sadness, comrades bound by a bond greater than that of so-called "family."

"Hm, is it that late?" he muttered to himself. All this wandering around and eating had dulled his sense of time, and he hadn't realized it was already lunchtime.

He looked for a place to set down the skewers in his right hand. Unable to find one, he shoved them all into the mountain of popcorn, and then dug around in his pocket to pull out an adorable stuffed fox toy with nine fluffy tails.

"Sorry for the wait." He set the popcorn down at his feet and took a food pill in his left hand.

The stuffed fox swallowed this down as though it were real food. "Yum! Yum!"

"Heh heh. Oh yeah?"

"Gimme more! More!"

"No need to rush. No one's gonna take it from you. You're my family, and I love you."

He made a point of learning about things his students were interested in whenever possible, which was why he'd purchased this Nine Tails Kuraa-ma, but he'd ended up deeply taken with it, surprisingly. Already, he doted on it in a ridiculous manner, so much so that he didn't hesitate to call it his family.

"My Kuraa-ma's much more clever and cuter than Naruto's Kurama. Heh heh...heh heh heh." Shino smiled fondly, the picture of a devoted father, while the insects in his chest clamored ever more loudly.

Two minutes later, they grew impatient of waiting on a host who was failing to provide their lunchtime chakra and began to greedily devour it without permission, causing Shino to faint.

FATHER AND DAUGHTER, FORMS OF HAPPINESS

2

The day before Family Day, while everyone else in Konohaga-kure was excitedly preparing for the holiday, in one corner of the village, Uzumaki Hinata hurriedly slipped through the gate to the Hyuga main house, the place where she'd been born. Without stopping to tidy the sandals she kicked off in the entryway, she raced intently down the hallway, wooden floorboards creaking.

She didn't hesitate as she made her way through the enormous house, turning corner after corner until she caught sight of her younger sister. "Hanabi?!"

"Hinata." Hanabi was crumpled on the floor in front of closed *shoji* doors, covering her mouth with the sleeve of her kimono, as if to hide a face swollen from crying.

That morning, a messenger had come to tell Hinata that their father, Hyuga Hiashi, had collapsed. She'd wanted to rush to his side right then and there, but faced with Hi-mawari, she'd been at a loss for words. How on earth was she supposed to tell her still-young daughter that it might be time for her to say goodbye to her grandfather? Unable to bring herself to have that conversation just yet, Hinata left the house alone without telling anyone the details of the situation.

She'd been spurred on by her own worry, but now that she'd made it to her family home, her heart froze at the sight of the weeping Hanabi, as though an icicle had been plunged into her chest.

"H-how's Father?" she asked in a trembling voice.

Hanabi glanced at the sliding doors—at their father's room—out of the corner of her eye. But she quickly dropped her head and averted her gaze. "Not great. He's been moaning and groaning this whole time. He says his body won't do what he wants."

"That's..." A shiver ran up Hinata's spine.

Their father, the very picture of Spartan living, had always been strict with his daughters, with fellow students, and with his own self. To protect the Hyuga name and all it stood for, he trained incessantly with almost obsessive devotion. He insisted that failing health was proof of a lack of discipline of the physical body. Not only had he never fallen ill, he had never so much as bent a knee to another person. Impossible to think that such a man would take to his sickbed now.

"So." Hanabi whirled her head around, anxiously trying to see behind Hinata. "Where's Boruto? He's not with you?"

"He's on a mission until this evening," Hinata replied. "Hey, what about the doctor? What'd the doctor say?"

"Doctor? Oh, the doctor." Hanabi stared off into space. "Umm, she said to put a cold pack on it and rest for now."

"A cold pack?" Hinata frowned. "Is all this because of a fever?"

Hinata felt something off in Hanabi's attitude, but before she could wonder further, her sister shot another question at her: "So what about Himawari?"

"I didn't know what to tell her," she mumbled. "So I left her at home."

"What? So then you came home all by yourself? What's that about?" Hanabi sprawled out, arms and legs splayed on the floor.

Hinata was ready to ask her the same thing. "Hey, Hanabi? Is this maybe…"

Krk, krk, krk. A sound like a walnut being crushed. Veins popped up around Hinata's white eyes, a new iris springing up in the center as a snowy white light radiated outward.

That light came from her Byakugan, a powerful technique passed down through the Hyuga clan. The Byakugan could see through all things, including the flow and nature of the chakra coursing through a human body. With this ocular jutsu, Hinata could see in essentially all directions, even detecting a soldier hiding several hundred meters away. And of course, she could see through walls as well. In the face of the Byakugan, the thin paper of the shoji doors might as well have been invisible.

Hinata turned toward her father's room. She peered through the shoji and saw him laid out on a futon in the center of a room covered in tatami mats. Feeling a pang of guilt at turning the Byakugan on her own father, she stared at him intently. There was nothing wrong with his lungs or his digestive organs. His blood circulated unhindered, and his liver was also the picture of health, perhaps because he hated heavy drinking. Only the muscles from his back down into his hips were a little tense.

"Father's…" Hinata stared at Hanabi with her white eyes. There was no need to use the Byakugan. Her younger sister was not actually crying. "He just threw out his back, didn't he?"

"Yes," Hanabi replied curtly, and began to kick and flail on the floor. "Aah, aah. And here I thought I'd finally get to see my adorable nephew and niiiiiece!"

"So you…" Hinata started. "You know, it's not okay to lie about—"

"Father *did* collapse," Hanabi cut her off. "And he's making a fool of himself fainting in agony over some back pain."

This was a side of her father she had never seen before. Still, when she realized his life was in no particular danger, Hinata felt the dark thing stuck in her chest melt away. She took one deep breath after another as she slumped down to the ground.

"And while I'm at it," Hanabi said. She had pulled herself into a sitting position and now pointed at their father's room. "Father's actually the one who wanted to see Boruto and Himawari, you know. He kept going on and on about how he could never face them in this condition, but then he was asking me if they'd really be all that upset seeing him like this. Or how he could comfort them if they did cry. He keeps grumbling and muttering and dithering. He could just *say* he wants them to come over."

Their father had always been strict, both with his daughters and with himself. But there were exceptions—or rather, one exception. And that was when it came to his grandchildren. The stern master of the house vanished the second they walked through the door. He was unbelievably doting every time he saw them, calling to them in a soft, coaxing voice, hugging them, pinching their cheeks, patting their heads like he thought the sun rose and set on them.

When Hinata was a child, she hadn't had the greatest relationship with her father. With her chunin exam, the distance between them had closed to some extent, but this was still a change she never dreamed she'd see in him.

"He might spoil those kids," Hinata muttered, slowly. "But I guess he'll never spoil us."

"Exactly how long are you going to stand out there whispering?" came their father's voice from inside his room.

Unconsciously, Hinata straightened up, and Hanabi stuck out her tongue.

"Fine, okay, we're coming." Hanabi opened the sliding door, and Hinata saw their father was sitting up in his futon.

She hadn't seen him for a while. His hair had gotten grayer as he'd aged, but the sharp light in his eyes and the intimidating air around him hadn't diminished at all. Why did that all go out the window the second he saw his grandchildren?

Like Hanabi, her father kept glancing behind her. "Where's Boruto? Himawari's not with you?" he asked impatiently.

With a sigh, Hinata settled down beside him. "I'm by myself. I hurried over, so."

"Is that so?" Even out of the corner of her eye, she could clearly see her father's shoulders slump. His posture practically screamed that she alone was not enough, and she felt the tiniest bit of indignation bite into her.

But now that I'm here looking at him up close…

Before she could put the feelings welling up in her heart into words, Hanabi leaned over and whispered into her ear, "You're thinking Father's gotten old, aren't you?"

Bull's-eye. Hinata was hard-pressed for a reply, however, and Hanabi brought her face in even closer.

"I think that's probably because of you."

"What do you mean?" Hinata was startled.

"You call him 'grandfather' now when Boruto and Himawari are around, right? I think that's sort of put the idea in his mind, you know? Like, 'Oh, right, I'm an old man now.' He's started using old man words when he talks, too."

"That's…" she tried to protest.

"Can you prove that's not it?" Hanabi stared at her intently.

Hinata was at a loss. Her father was getting old because of her? The thought had never so much as crossed her mind.

"Both of you. You can't possibly have that much to sit around and whisper about." Hiashi chuckled now that he had recovered from the shock of his grandchildren's absence, utterly ignorant of his daughters' concerns. "Sorry for worrying you, Hinata."

"Honestly," she sighed. "You could've just said you threw out your back."

"What? It's obviously embarrassing." He frowned. "It's much more difficult than you'd imagine to admit you're old."

Old. Feeling a pinch of discomfort at the word, Hinata averted her eyes. She turned instead to Hanabi. Her younger sister grinned like a child who had successfully pulled off a prank. She didn't say a thing out loud, but Hinata read the message in her playful eyes loud and clear: *So you finally noticed?* She wanted to rebut her sister, but her father opened his mouth before she could.

"And how is Naruto then? I heard he's as busy as ever."

"Y-yes," she stammered. "He hasn't even been able to come home lately."

"So then—" Hiashi started to say, and then suddenly cut himself off. He fell silent, as if feigning a nonchalance, and closed his eyes, the furrow between his brows growing deeper.

Hinata watched him, puzzled. Unlike Hanabi's easy-to-read face, she had no idea what her father was trying to say.

Finally, he opened his eyes again. "And how are Boruto and Himawari?" he asked with a smile, changing the subject and the mood in the room.

Her discomfort was still gnawing at her, but she couldn't exactly bring the age question back up. "Himawari's sad her dad hasn't been coming home. But she understands that he has to work. Boruto is…" *Hanging out with friends on genin missions. Fighting with his father.* There were too many ways to finish that sentence, and she struggled with where to start.

Hanabi took her silence to mean something else. "Getting to be time for him to strike out on his own. Isn't that sad for you?"

"No, that's…" She tried to deny it but ended up trailing off.

"Uh? No way!" Hanabi cried. "I hit the nail on the head?"

"He's *not* leaving home," Hinata protested. "He's still a child and a real handful. It's just… Lately, he's been buying things with his own money, and I'm a little worried…"

"Well, of course he's going to buy things now that he's getting paid for missions," Hanabi said. "It's sort of ridiculous to get an allowance from your parents forever. So what'd he start buying? Snacks? Video games?"

"Underpants," Hinata replied.

"U—" Hanabi froze with her mouth open on the "u," but then quickly broke into a wide smile and began to laugh loudly. "Ha ha ha ha ha ha ha! What is *that* about?! You're getting worried about a thing like *that*?! About something as simple as Boruto buying his own underpants?!"

"It's just, the colors he chooses are kind of off," she protested. "Like, fluorescent pink, you know?"

"He's got good taste." Her sister shrugged.

"When I peek into his room at night, his butt will be glowing in the dark."

"That's very Boruto." Hanabi wiped away tears from laughing too hard.

Hinata patted her cheek, a troubled look on her face, but then stopped abruptly. Her father had pulled a notebook out of his pocket and was writing something down. She narrowed her eyes. Even without the Byakugan, she could pick up the details: "Boruto likes fluorescent pink."

"Father." She cleared her throat as if admonishing him. Her father didn't only express his love through excessive and overbearing physical contact; he also tried to capture their hearts with presents. If she didn't set him straight right away, her whole house might end up fluorescent pink.

But it appeared she was just a tiny bit too late. Her father turned toward her sister and asked, "Was there anything fluorescent pink in the presents we bought for today?"

"I'm not sure. Hmm." Hanabi headed for a corner of the room.

Hinata gulped in surprise when she saw the mountain of presents wrapped in colorful paper that filled the decorative *tokonoma* alcove. Incredible. She stared at her father, dumbfounded.

"Got a bit carried away." He rubbed his hip, seeming embarrassed. "Just happened to end up like this once we put them all together in one place."

That wasn't exactly the answer she'd been looking for, but before she could say anything, she heard the *krk krk* of Hanabi using her Byakugan.

"Hmm. Nope, nothing. It's all black or grey. And brown. Dark brown.

"What about the sweets?" he asked.

"Those are…black and tea green. And brown and dark brown." Hanabi frowned. "Father, did you really need to buy so many *senbei* crackers? You got doubles here with the rich soy and plain soy flavors."

"Boruto and Himawari might end up fighting over them if I don't have one for each," their father noted, ever serious.

Hinata's head started to hurt. She pressed her fingers to her temples.

Fluorescent pink snacks were far too disturbing to give to her children, and at any rate, they were not going to start a fight over senbei of all things. The presents her father selected were always off somehow. Exactly like Boruto thinking that fluorescent pink was cool.

"I think maybe the kids…probably don't really want fluorescent pink toys and snacks." While she was at it, she added in a small voice, "Or senbei."

"Oh!" Her father crossed his arms, a complicated expression on his face. "Is that so? Well then, what *do* they want?"

She had expected this question, but she was still stuck for an answer. She didn't actually want to say anything when she thought about her house being buried in whatever she told him. But she couldn't lie, either. His heart was in the right place, after all. She wanted to respect that.

After struggling with the question, she had a flash of insight. "Actually. There *is* this thing Boruto's been obsessed with lately. This card game, what was it called…? Fierce Ninja? Something like that." She bit her lip, frustrated that she couldn't remember the name.

"Oh, X Cards?" Hanabi interjected unexpectedly.

Hiashi grew more solemn, more sternly handsome, perhaps because of the unfamiliar words. "Oh. A card game. X Cards."

"The proper name is Extreme Ninja. But everyone calls it X Cards. You play all these famous ninja—Oh! It's kind of like *hanafuda* cards," Hanabi explained smoothly.

Dumbfounded, Hinata stared at her sister. "You sure know a lot about it."

"Well, you know. It *is* popular and all. Hang on. I should have a few cards in my room." She stepped out into the hall without waiting for a reply.

Hinata noticed that her father's expression was as complicated as it had been earlier.

"Hmm," he said, the furrow between his brows disappearing as he felt her gaze on him. "About these X Cards or whatever they are… She said the game is about famous ninja, but what era of ninja exactly?"

"I think it covers shinobi from all times and places. I guess there's a Naruto card in there." Hinata shrugged. "But I don't think it's a great present. He'll just be disappointed if he doesn't get the cards he wants."

Each Extreme Ninja pack contained ten cards, but the only way to find out which ones was to open the pack, which meant that a player couldn't simply buy the particular card they had their eye on. In other words, the very act of buying Extreme Ninja cards was a gamble. Hinata had told Boruto until she was blue in the face that he shouldn't be doing anything remotely resembling gambling when he was still so young. But her son took no heed of her, and his room was scattered with doubles and other unwanted cards.

When she brought up Extreme Ninja, it was with an ulterior motive. She'd thought that if she told her father all this, he would put aside the idea of giving the cards as a present and join her in trying to get Boruto to stop playing the game in consideration of his grandson's future.

"That…is not so bad." Her father nodded, and Hinata realized she had missed the mark.

"Father? Are you actually listening to me? You can't know if the cards will be a hit. If you give him a bunch of misses, Boruto might end up even hating you, you know?" she said, half in threat, as she leaned in toward him.

But Hiashi was not ruffled in the least. "I realize that. However, I wouldn't necessarily simply give him packs of cards. If shinobi from all times and places are the theme, then one of those cards must be mine. I was thinking of getting one of *those* for Boruto." Her father seemed extremely pleased with himself.

Meanwhile, Hinata cradled her head in her hands at the hornet's nest she had stirred up.

"Okay." Hanabi came back in, carrying a binder. For all of her modesty about having "a few cards," the orange binder was quite thick. Small decorative jewels spelled out her name in glittering letters on the cover: "Ha♥na♥bi."

"H-Hanabi?" Hinata furrowed her brow in confusion. "You… That… You seem really into this. What's going on?"

"Oh, it's one of those things." Her sister shrugged. "Once you start collecting them, you just can't stop."

She sighed and rolled her eyes, utterly exasperated. To think that not only her son, but her sister and father even would be so interested in this gambling game.

"So? Let's have a look." Hiashi opened the binder. Each page had nine cards, the faces of various ninja lined up on them.

Hanabi pointed to one featuring the first Hokage, Senju Hashirama. "On the bottom right here is the rarity. So SSR is super special rare—Mm, I'm not sure how to explain it, Father. Maybe if these were hanafuda cards, this would be a *goko*, a run of five cards. And SR is super rare—*shiko*, a run of four. R is rare, the *sanko* of three. There's U and C, too, but those ones would be the easiest plays, I guess? Like *tan* or *kasu*."

Hinata noticed a "C" on the face of her former teammate Aburame Shino and suddenly she was done with the whole thing. Shino, a kasu card…

"I see." Their father nodded, knowingly. "The higher the role points, the rarer the card. I can see why Boruto likes it. So then where am I?"

"You're… Um, here." Hanabi flipped through the pages and stopped exactly one third of the way in. Pictured there was their youthful father.

However.

"Enough with the jokes, Hanabi." He turned to her with a bright smile that was unimaginable from the stern look on the card. "This says R. Boruto wouldn't want something so run-of-the-mill. If I'm going to give him one, it has to be an SSR me. Where is that one?"

Hanabi shook her head from side to side.

"What? You don't have it?" he asked.

She kept shaking her head.

"You can't mean..."

She said nothing and stared at their father. He stared back.

"Do you mean," he paused, pained, "I stop at R?"

Hanabi bobbed her head up and down.

"W—*Me*, the head of the Hyuga main house...a mere R? That's...that's ridiculous." With each word, the color drained from his face. "That such a thing would befall the Hyugas," he murmured, stupefied.

Unable to look directly at him anymore, Hinata averted her eyes. Hanabi apparently felt the same. Their eyes met in the place where they were averting them to. Again, she could tell right away what her sister wanted to say: *So which one of us is going to console him?* Then, almost as an afterthought, *You go ahead and do the honors.*

With no other choice, Hinata smiled faintly. "F-Father? Don't take it to heart. That's not what the village thinks. It's a children's game."

"Yes, right," Hanabi agreed. "It's just the company that makes the game, in the end. Boruto'll have a real laugh at your expense if you take it all so seriously."

Hiashi continued to stare out into empty space, heedless of his daughters' kind words. Hanabi waved a hand in front of his face to check if he was still with them.

Hinata heard a strange sound, like an insect's wings, and then realized that her father was the source.

He was whispering almost soundlessly. "...should I do?"

"What?" she asked.

"To become SSR...what should I do?"

Once again, Hinata and Hanabi frowned as they met each other's eyes. Their attempt to console him had been in vain; their father was going to be stubborn about this. She groped for some explanation, but what could she say to him when he was in this state? Not a single thing came to mind.

"When you look at the SSR people..." Hanabi turned the binder page reluctantly. "Well, it's an incredible line-up. The Kages, the Three Great Shinobi. I don't know the criteria they set for this, but I guess you'd just have to go out and do something as great as they did."

"So you're saying go find fame? To think at *this* age, I would be pressed into service." Their father laughed in self-deprecation.

A heavy, uncomfortable feeling lodged itself in the pit of Hinata's stomach as she sensed where the conversation was going. He couldn't possibly—

"I'll go to the Hokage and get a mission," he announced, standing up.

"Father?!"

"Faaather?!"

His daughters hurriedly followed their father to their feet and tried to stop him somehow.

"*Now*?" Hinata asked. "Please stop this foolishness."

"Honestly," Hanabi sighed. "The doctor said you were supposed to rest."

"Ha! This amount of pain is nothing at all." He moved to step out into the hall, clearly not interested in a word they had to say. He was putting on a brave act, but Hinata could see the awkward way he moved his legs.

"If something were to happen to you, Father, the children

would be sad, you know?" she said.

"They'll be much sadder if they find out that their own grandfather is an old dodderer who is nothing more than an R!" he shouted. "I must become SSR, no matter what it takes! To make my adorable grandchildren happy!"

"It's just a silly card game. You can't," Hanabi said. "Please, just think—"

"Enough!" He would obviously brook no further argument. He slammed the sliding doors together, a physical punctuation mark for emphasis.

Hinata groaned, while behind her Hanabi shrugged.

@ @ @ @ @

Hinata definitely couldn't just leave their father to run off on a half-baked mission, so, little sister in tow, she headed for the Hokage's office.

In front of the office door, Nara Shikamaru was scratching his head, looking annoyed. "I mean, you come in here out of the blue, demanding a mission, you know? Mission requests aren't even usually done here. That's what the counter at the front is for."

"The counter only handles the easy missions." As if to press the younger man for a reply, Hiashi took a step closer. "What I'm looking for is an extremely difficult mission. I don't care what it is. Guarding a VIP, transporting goods, I'm not fussy."

"Where is this coming from?" Shikamaru asked. "I mean, you're the head of the Hyuga main house."

"I simply decided I needed to keep my skills up. Enough with all these questions."

Shikamaru clearly wasn't going to swallow this explanation wholesale. "An extremely difficult mission for the sake of your skills? You're quite confident there." His sarcasm was clear in both his voice and his gaze. He was too busy for this kind of bother.

Hinata was on tenterhooks, but her sister could not have looked more carefree. The corners of her mouth relaxing into a grin, she whispered in Hinata's ear, "I guess he's still got enough sense in his head to care about what other people think since he's not coming straight out and saying he wants to increase the rarity of his card."

"I guess you're right. But I never thought he'd try to get a mission directly from Naruto." Hinata sighed. He was in charge of the most difficult missions the village of Konohaga-kure was hired for. And those were what their father had his sights set on.

Hiashi paused. "If I say I just dropped by to see my son-in-law, would you let me through?"

"Unfortunately, the Lord Seventh has his hands full at the moment. That's why I'm here talking to you, sir." *What a hassle*—the words were clearly written on Shikamaru's face.

Hinata wondered whether she should tell her father to come back another day, but then something Shikamaru said caught her attention. "Is Naruto busy?"

"Hm? Yeah. Not sure if he'll be able to make it home toda—" Shikamaru started and then seemed to realized he had slipped. He cut himself off and clicked his tongue instead. "Nah, I mean, he's busy, but it's a thing he'll finish up today. He's really looking forward to Family Day tomorrow. Don't worry. He'll be home tonight."

His sudden change of tune didn't entirely eliminate Hinata's unease. She was expecting Naruto to come home. That's why she'd left Himawari there. •

Naruto, you are coming home, right? She stared at the closed door of his office with worried eyes.

"So about the mission." Shikamaru dropped his gaze to the clipboard in his hand, as if to flee the awkward moment. "Would it just be you, sir? Or..."

"Of course, just—"

Hanabi stepped forward to brush Hiashi aside and held up three fingers. "A three-person cell."

"Hanabi?" father and older sister said at the same time.

Hanabi turned first to their father. "I know you've been training without a break, Father. I know that better than anyone. But it's been too long since you were in the field. A single- person mission with no backup is maybe too much."

"Hmm." Hiashi couldn't really argue given that it was his sparring partner Hanabi saying this.

Then Hanabi shifted her gaze, but Hinata was ready with her argument.

"If we're talking time out of the field, it's also been quite a while for me."

"True." Her younger sister nodded. "It might be a lot for you after ten or however many years as a housewife. But you'd worry if Father went out on his own, right?"

"Well...that's true, but..." What she really wanted at this moment, when it was uncertain if her husband would actually leave the office that day, was to make her apologies to her father and sister and go straight home for the sake of her children. But when she was about to confess these feelings, Hanabi's words back at the house wedged themselves in her throat, preventing her from speaking.

You're thinking Father's gotten old, aren't you?

I think that's probably because of you.

"Well, what if you help out and spend some time with your father?" Shikamaru seemed to take her silence as consent, rather than her desperately reaching for some way to get out of going anywhere, and he began to tell them at length the details of the mission.

"So a group of Byakugan users then… Okay. A developer breaking ground in the Konoha onsen area called us early this morning. Seems like someone stole the explosives they use for excavation work and then took off. The site's full of steam, so they can't see anything at all, which makes it hard to go after the thief. But that shouldn't be an issue for the Byakugan. This page has a map and the other details…"

@ @ @ @ @

"I shouldn't have come," Hanabi complained at the onsen area, a half day's journey from the Hokage's office, even though she was the one who had taken the lead in putting them in that place. "What is that *smell*? Like rotten eggs. Aah, seriously. I really like this kimono. My best kimono'll be ruined if that stink settles into the fabric."

"You should have changed then," Hinata chided her sister as she trailed along behind her, but she too cringed at the strange, persistent stink that found its way into her mouth no matter how shallow her breaths. Plus, the area was a rocky zone untouched by any human hand and made slippery by the steam. Not to mention that the hills were painfully steep. And so…

"Eeaaah!" Her feet quickly went out from under. She flung her hands up to try and maintain her balance and ended up slapping Hanabi hard in the face.

"Ack!" her sister cried.

"I-I'm sorry."

"And you, Hinata, why are you in sandals?!" Hanabi groaned, tearfully, holding her nose.

Just as Shikamaru had told them at the office, geysers erupted all over the area, blanketing the world in steam and coloring their field of view a snowy white. They were just barely able to make headway thanks to the Byakugan, but her eyes were gradually getting more and more tired.

"Up ahead's no good. We'll have to detour." In the lead, their father started them off in yet another direction.

"Again?" Hanabi reproached him. "Father, we've just been going round and round in circles, haven't we?"

"If you don't like it, you can leave," he sniffed. "If we keep going straight, we'll be waking up in the afterlife in seconds."

On top of everything else, clouds of natural poisonous gas drifted about, meaning they couldn't simply march forward the way they would have liked to.

Hanabi seemed to be pouting, but perhaps accepting that their father's decision was the right one, she didn't question him further. Instead, she started complaining again. "Honestly. What's this thief doing running off into a place like this? It stinks, it's hot, it's humid, and if you're not careful, you'll die. I would think this is basically the worst place in the world for a hideout."

"Maybe they thought it would be good for hiding precisely because no one comes here," Hinata suggested.

"If they're just going to hide, then sure," Hanabi assented. "But what about after that?"

"After?" She paused. "Shikamaru said the thief might use the stolen explosives for terrorism."

"So then they'll have to head down to the village again, right?" her sister said. "In which case, they should've looked for an abandoned building there to use as a hideout instead of running off into this nightmare of a place."

Hinata assumed her sister was just grumbling about the thief, but that was apparently not the case.

"I mean, he said explosives, but the ones they use for excavation can't be *that* powerful," Hanabi noted. "Would you risk your life for something like that? And *we* can walk around here because of who we are, but most people'd be dead already, y'know?"

"They're doing research into all kinds of scientific ninja tools lately," Hinata said. "Maybe there's one to detect smoke and poison."

"But if they had access to stuff like that, they wouldn't be stealing a bunch of pathetic explosives. And why wouldn't they use some super explosive created with the full might of science? Something's off here," Hanabi concluded.

"Both of you, that's enough chitchat," their father said, looking ahead.

Hinata also focused her Byakugan and saw human silhouettes in the steam about forty meters ahead. Three, just like her group. All were equipped with ostentatious masks with cylindrical filters. It seemed that the detours their father had taken them on had brought them into contact with the thief—no, thieves, sooner than initially expected.

"Poison... None. I'll take the one in the center. Hanabi, you're on the right. Hinata, the left. Let's go," their father instructed, and dashed into the curtain of steam.

Sweat sprang up on the palms of her hands. She still trained with Boruto at the house, but it had been a long time since she'd seen actual combat. But there was no time to hesitate. She had to go after her father right away.

Hiashi had no sooner leaped out in front of them than their opponents were crying out in bewilderment. "Huh? Wha— Who are you?!"

"No questions. This is for the sake of my grandchildren. Ready yourself!" Hiashi spread his legs apart and hunkered down deeply.

"Art of the Gentle Fist! Eight Trigrams Sixty-Four Palms!"

He bundled his fingertips together and stepped toward his opponent. "Eight Trigrams Two Palms!"

"Gah?!"

Three hundred sixty-one "tenketsu" chakra points existed within the body. "Four Palms!"

"Hngah!"

Hiashi saw all of them with the Byakugan. "Eight Palms!"

"Bah!"

His speed belied his age. "Thirty-Two Palms!"

"Znrh!!"

He pierced each chakra point with unerring precision. "Sixty-Four Palms!"

"Bwah?!"

The opponent, powerless against the essence of the Gentle Fist, was sent flying. The gas mask came off her face and carved a clean arc out in the air.

Hiashi looked down on his opponent, who was unable to even scream in agony as she convulsed and twitched. "Did you see that? Hyuga is the strongest in all of Konoha! Best remember that."

However.

Perhaps sensing eyes on him, Hiashi looked around suspiciously.

Hanabi sighed. In a panic, Hinata was racing over to the opponent he'd knocked flying. The two opponents his daughters were supposed to have taken care of were glaring at him, and the expressions beneath their masks were fierce.

Hanabi gently pointed to the armband one was wearing around his shoulder. *Permission to excavate Konoha onsen*, it read.

He'd seen the tenketsu clearly, but in his great hurry to please his grandchildren, Hiashi had overlooked something even more important.

＠ ＠ ＠ ＠ ＠

"Aah," Hanabi moaned. "It *is* settling in."

"Hanabi," Hinata snapped. "Stop sniffing at your kimono like an animal. It's indecent."

It was past midnight. They were walking toward the foot of the onsen town after coming down from the rocky zone. The distinctive scent also rose up from the river that ran alongside the road, but it was almost pleasant compared with the stench in the highlands earlier. This, indeed, was the fragrant aroma of the onsen.

"Whatever. It's all in your clothes too, right? And I mean, Father—" Hanabi started and then looked around. Their father was gone. "Father? Oh, there he is!"

Far in the distance behind them, he trudged along, shoulders slumped. Sorrow oozed like chakra from his entire body.

Hanabi's face clouded over as if under the spell of this malaise. "Well, it's no wonder."

Hiashi had taken down the developer who hired them for the mission in the first place. It turned out the mission information itself had been mistaken. The explosives hadn't actually been stolen; it had been a mere miscount. The perpetrator who had supposedly fled inland was just an incorrectly identified tourist sneaking in for a soak at the source. Although an apology had been sent to the Hokage's office with a request to cancel the mission, it was already too late. The Hyuga family had already marched up into the mountains, just missing the messenger.

Since everyone involved had made a mistake, the developers were turning a blind eye to the whole thing, fortunately. But Hiashi was utterly dejected. If he couldn't fulfill his objective of carrying out a difficult mission, he couldn't make Boruto happy, either.

"Well, that *was* a sorry excuse for a mission. But to think that Father would just charge in like that without double-checking who was ahead!" Hanabi cried out. "Why did we even come along?"

"Shh!" Hinata held a finger to her lips. "He's upset enough. You don't have to go on and on about it."

"Fine. But he can't hear us. He's stuck way back there."

And indeed, their father was lagging far behind. It would take a while for him to catch up.

"So what do you want to do? Find a hotel or something?" Hanabi asked while they waited.

"I'd like to head home right now if I could." Hinata frowned. "I just know Naruto's going to be late, and I didn't leave supper for the kids."

"You'll never make it now. I know you're worried about Himawari and Boruto, but you could walk all night without stopping, and it'd still be morning before you got there." Hanabi chuckled, knowingly. "And anyway, I already told Boruto you'd be gone, so."

"Whaaat?!" Hinata shrieked.

"I told him to work something out for supper. He was just happy he got to play video games for as long as he wanted."

"But...just the kids alone..."

"How about you trust them a little bit?" Hanabi suggested, archly. "He *is* buying underpants on his own now."

"That's got nothing to do with this," she protested. "I have to watch out for those kids of mine."

"Aah! Come on!" Her sister's eyes glittered dangerously. "Face reality. You can't go home today. Boruto and Himawari are fine. And I want to soak in the onsen." She waved a smelly kimono sleeve and emphasized each and every word as though teaching a baby how to talk. "And this is a hot spring cure for

Father. We came all the way to the onsen, after all. You also have to make time for yourself sometimes, Hinata."

Before she could respond, Hanabi moved the conversation forward on her own. Shading her eyes with a hand, she glanced around at the nearby inns. "Hmm. How about that one? Looks good, anyway."

Eventually, they settled on a place and went over to ask about rooms. The sign hanging outside read *Shika no Tsuno Onsen*.

"Oh!" Hinata said, the instant she laid eyes on it.

"What?" Hanabi turned to look at her. "You don't like it?"

"Huh? Oh, no. It's not that."

"Yeah? Okay, so there." Hanabi just pushed her sister's objections aside as she turned toward their father, still lagging some ways back on the road. "Faaather? We're going to the onseeeen! Hurry uuuuup! The water'll get coooooold!"

It was unclear whether or not the word *onsen* had any effect, but their father's pace did increase ever so slightly.

◎　◎　◎　◎　◎

Plnk! The wooden bucket hit the floor in the large outdoor bath, which was surrounded by a wall of trees. The woman finished rinsing off and headed for the changing room, leaving only Hinata and Hanabi behind in the bath, perhaps because of the already late hour.

"Heh heh. It's like we have our own private bath here." Hair tied up on top of her head, Hanabi leaned back against the edge and stretched out, her skin making a somehow satisfying squeaking sound against the wall of the tub. "This feels so good, mmm..."

"I guess not too many people are staying here tonight."

Hinata rubbed her legs under the hot water. Her joints were stiff and sore, perhaps from too much walking. She looked up at the starry sky peeking out over the edge of the rain eave. "Maybe they've all got rooms in town because of tomorrow. Family Day."

"So, Hinata?" Hanabi stretched a hand down into the water, and *plsh*! Wavelets rippled outward. "What do you remember when you think about family?"

"What?" Hinata furrowed her brow. "I have lots of memories. Like Boruto's birthday or—"

"No, not that. I'm not talking about Boruto and Himawari. I mean, memories of Father."

"Of Father?"

"Especially from when we were little. Got anything?"

Hinata dropped her gaze to the water's surface and stared at her own face wobbling in the waves, but not a single thing came to mind. Although she thought about it until the waves died down, she still couldn't come up with an answer.

"Training, I guess," she said, finally.

"I *knew* it. Me, too." Hanabi sounded embarrassed somehow. "Like, training in the breaks from training. It was totally normal for us, so I didn't think much of it. But, I mean, he never took us to play anywhere."

"He was so focused on protecting the Hyuga family and Konoha," Hinata agreed.

"Yeah. It's not like I especially hated it, though. I like training. But..." Hanabi paused. "When I see how good Naruto is with Boruto and Himawari, it's like, maybe Father was going too far or something."

Hinata took this in. "I guess. Father's... He seems happier now."

"Took the words out of my mouth!"

Giggling, the sisters exchanged a grin. Eventually, their

laughter died down, and silence fell over the outdoor bath. Only the quiet sound of the water pumping in reached Hinata's ears. She gave herself over to the warmth of the water for a while.

"So, like..." Hanabi opened her mouth again after what seemed like careful deliberation. "After you said how busy the Lord Hokage was, Father started to say something. 'So then.' Remember?"

"Yes." Hinata remembered right away. "He suddenly got so quiet. I thought it was weird."

"Want me to tell you what he was going to say?" Hanabi slid over to Hinata, parting the water before her. They were so close their shoulders were touching as Hanabi peered into her sister's face. "'So then how about you bring Boruto and Himawari home with you until things settle down for the Lord Hokage.' *That's* what he was going to say."

"What?" Go to her family home with her children? She was taken utterly off guard and all she could do was stare at her sister, frozen.

"It's hard for you to look after Boruto and Himawari all by yourself," Hanabi said. "And Father would be over the moon if he could live with his beloved grandchildren. I don't think it's such a bad idea."

"Not bad? So you think I should, too?"

"If it will make Father happy, I'm all for it," Hanabi declared . She snapped her mouth shut and waited intently for an answer.

But there was no way Hinata could simply decide something like that on the spur of the moment.

A hint of despair crept into her sister's white eyes. "You don't want to?"

"I want to help for Father's sake, but..." Hinata trailed off.

"He seems happier now than he used to," Hanabi remarked.

"You said so yourself."

"I did, but… I mean, you springing this on me, how am I supposed to…"

"What?"

Silence once more.

Hanabi's despair wasn't just in her eyes now; it spread to her whole body. "This is going nowhere," she said in a strained voice, and stepped out of the bath. She wound a towel around herself, and Hinata heard a familiar sound. *Krk, krk.*

"Let's settle this right now." Hanabi looked down on her with Byakugan eyes. "We fight, Hinata. If I win, you come home."

"What are you—here? Don't be silly." Hinata tried to smooth things over, but she knew looking at Hanabi that this was no joke. She was dead serious, a fact that came through loud and clear. Her little sister meant business.

"What? You afraid you'll lose?" Hanabi challenged.

Hinata was at a loss for words.

"Still not talking? C'mon. Get ready. Hurry up."

Reluctantly, Hinata got out of the bath and wrapped a towel around herself. With her eyes, she asked, *Do we really have to do this?* But her sister's will was firm, unshakeable. With no other choice, Hinata focused her power in her eyes, bringing out her Byakugan, and faced Hanabi.

She remembered how they sparred when they were little. Mock battles in the courtyard of the main house with the Hyuga family watching over them. Back then, her little sister had been the better strategist, and their father had given up on Hinata, a talentless shinobi. But her trip down memory lane didn't last long.

Hanabi came flying at her without a word or any starting signal. The heel of her sister's palm drove in at her. She parried with one arm and dodged the striking hand that followed with her other. Hanabi whirled around and launched a sword hand at her, but Hinata sank down and dodged it by a hair's breadth.

The chakra imbued in each and every blow was so great that one direct hit could decide the whole fight.

Hinata struck out with a hand, too, and no sooner had her sister dodged this than she was sweeping out for a kick to knock Hanabi to the floor.

Perhaps judging that she wouldn't be able to completely absorb this kick, Hanabi threw herself backward, then took a step to get even more distance between them.

Hinata saw her opportunity and stepped forward with a palm strike. But Hanabi brushed it aside with a fist, knocking her off balance. Her sister didn't miss the chance to counterattack with another palm strike.

"Ngh!" Hinata just barely managed to dodge, but if Hanabi kept charging her like this, she wouldn't be able to avoid the next hit. She thrust her palm out in a sweeping stroke, a single blow at the chin.

Hanabi twisted her head to avoid the strike, but the force of Hinata's blow kicked up a sudden gust that pulled her hair down from where it was tied up on top of her head. Brownish-black hair flew out around her, and she leapt backward, perhaps impeded by the sudden halo of hair.

Neither of them was breathing hard, but Hinata was frustrated. She was duller than when she's been on active duty and working missions.

Hanabi couldn't have been going easy on her because of this, and indeed, her little sister opened her mouth and dispelled any doubt she might have had. "I'm surprised. I planned to decide this on the first blow. You're still pretty sharp, huh, Hinata?"

"When it comes to the basics...I've been teaching Boruto at home."

"Makes sense. Boruto came over to check, y'know, whether or not the Byakugan had manifested. So I did a little sparring with him then. Nothing hard. He wasn't too bad."

"You sparred with Boruto?" Hinata cried. "What were you thinking? He's still a child!"

"He's not a child," Hanabi pronounced, crisply. "He's getting genin missions. His physical techniques are on par with any adult's. It's not that he's not trying to set out on his own, it's that you can't let him go. Isn't that right, Hinata?"

"You..." She was at a loss for words.

"Can you really say I'm wrong?" her sister said, as if returning to the conversation at the house, although all trace of the mischievousness she'd seen on Hanabi's face then had completely vanished. "It's the same as Father becoming Grandfather. Time marches forward. And that boy, he's growing up. How about you accept it already? I think that would make Boruto happy."

Hinata stared at her wordlessly. She'd thought her children would be children forever. They'd come to her in tears when they skinned their knees, they'd crawl into her futon with her when they had a scary dream. But Boruto had already stopped crying in front of her. He wasn't frightened of scary dreams anymore. He was...

He's not a child anymore?

Suddenly, she remembered what her father had said at the house.

It's much more difficult than you'd imagine to admit you're old.

That was exactly it, she thought. Time flowed, and Boruto moved away from her. She hadn't wanted to accept it, so she'd pretended she didn't see it. Pretended he would forever be a child who needed her.

"And...I don't just want Father and Boruto to be happy." Hanabi started to close the distance between them once more.

Hinata stepped forward at the ready, but her sister was already ten steps ahead. Right hand, left hand—one palm strike after another.

"I want that for you, too, Hinata!"

After dodging the strikes, Hinata dropped down and tried to sweep Hanabi's feet out from under her, but her sister leaped up to somehow evade her and then dropped down from the sky, kicking.

"Me?!" She crossed her arms and managed to catch her sister's leg somehow. The shock shuddered through her very bones. Unconsciously, she stiffened up.

"The Hokage promised. On your wedding day, he promised to make you happy!" Hanabi bounced up from where she'd landed and charged Hinata, fists flying.

Hinata just barely managed to keep from being hit, but then a palm strike flew in, catching her unawares.

"But he didn't keep that promise, did he?!" Hanabi shouted as she launched a roundhouse from behind to sweep Hinata's feet out from under her, while still attacking relentlessly with her hands, and then shot out with a dizzying succession of kicks.

Hinata practically fell over backward, but she managed to dodge somehow. Still, her narrow escape left no room to counterattack, and she was forced to keep retreating.

"He's too busy with the Hokage work, and he never comes home." Without hesitation, Hanabi swooped in closer and dropped down, ready to strike with her hands again. "If he saw the house empty, his family gone..."

Hinata wouldn't be able to escape this one unscathed. She braced herself and got ready to strike.

"Then maybe he would actually pay attention to his family!"

In the next instant, the sisters' blows slammed against each other. The air itself ripped apart and echoed in the deserted bath area. Neither of their hands had hit home; instead, they'd slipped off to the sides, but now that their arms were crossed up against each other, neither sister could move. They were too close to each other to launch another blow.

Her sister a heartbeat away from her, Hinata stared into her eyes. She thought that this would be enough to see what her sister was feeling, and in fact, it was. But she couldn't believe her sister was so upset about this.

"You're wrong, Hanabi," Hinata whispered.

"How am I wrong?!" Hanabi glanced at Hinata's side with stern eyes. Perhaps seeing an opening there, she swept aside their deadlocked arms and lashed out with a palm strike.

But Hinata had left herself open as bait. She twisted around and dodged the blow with a flowing movement before striking down Hanabi's outstretched arm.

"Aah—?!" Her sister fell forward, her back defenseless.

Hinata hesitated for an instant. But then she slammed her arm down onto her sister's back.

"Ow!" Hanabi hit the wooden floor face first.

Hinata let out a long sigh. Not at her sister, but rather a sigh of relief that the contest had finally been decided. "That's my win... Yeah?"

Holding her nose, Hanabi turned partway toward her. She'd released her Byakugan, but her eyes looked resentful. Still, she didn't protest Hinata's decision. Instead, she asked, in a teary voice, "How am I wrong?"

Hinata looked around the outdoor bath. "Here. This onsen. Shika no Tsuno Onsen. I have a lot of memories in this place." She smiled fondly. "I came here on my honeymoon with Naruto. Hee hee! He hasn't changed a bit since then."

Hanabi was sulking, utterly uninterested, but Hinata paid her no mind.

"Some memories take shape and stick with you, and some

don't. Places, memories. Do you want to forget your time training with Father?"

"Sometimes," Hanabi admitted. "Like, the days when he would yell at me because I wasn't getting any better."

"But all of it?"

"Well…" Hanabi fell silent, but that was an answer in and of itself, and she knew that just as well as Hinata did.

"For Boruto and Himawari, all their memories right now are in that house. The sunflower seeds we planted in the garden, the notches in the wall to record how tall they are. Those…" She hesitated, but then steeled herself to continue. "Those memories are important, a time when Boruto was a child who needed me. That's why I can't come home."

Hanabi looked sad at this.

"And, you know…" Her cheeks were cool from the evaporated bath water, but now she felt them warm ever so slightly. "You're right, Hanabi. Naruto *is* busy. But he's absolutely keeping his promise. I'm happy. I've always been. I feel the same way as I did when we were here on our honeymoon." A gentle smile played on her lips. "Because I love Naruto—"

"Oh, enough. Stop. I get it. Don't make me listen to you gush about him." Hanabi sounded entirely unamused as she plugged her ears. She even squeezed her eyes shut tightly, not even wanting to look at her sister's flushed cheeks. "Once you get started on the lovey-dovey stuff, you never stop. Seriously. Makes my ears hurt."

"Ouch. You don't have to go that far…"

"Well… If you're happy, I guess it's fine." She said this too quietly for Hinata to hear, though.

"What did you say?" Hinata asked.

"Nothing." Hanabi let out an exaggerated sigh and moved toward the tub. "I got all worked up for nothing. I'm totally chilled to the bone. Maybe I'll jump back in the bath. You should warm up, too, Hi—Ah!"

Perhaps because her eyes were still shut, her foot got caught on the edge of the tub, and she fell forward into the bath. A huge plume of water splashed up, and drops of bath water flew everywhere.

@ @ @ @ @

"Father? Are you going to sulk about this forever?"

The following day they set out on the road back to the village, which would no doubt be busy with Family Day. Hiashi's shoulders were still slumped, but he seemed a bit better. He was keeping up with them now, at least.

Whether she liked it or not, Hinata could hear her father and sister talking behind her.

"Don't hang your head like that. You'll fall if you're not careful. Like a certain someone yesterday. You don't have to try so hard. You don't have to get Boruto X Cards. You can get him something else, like senbei. With the double punch of rich soy and regular soy, he'll be in heaven."

"Actually," their father said.

Hinata stopped, and her father and sister did the same.

"I was thinking about this yesterday when I was soaking in the bath alone. Those things are really just tea cakes for old people. I need to give them something a younger tongue would enjoy."

Hanabi was stunned into silence, but quickly recovered and urged him to continue. "So then? So?"

"Let's see. Hamburgers...perhaps?" He raised a doubtful eyebrow.

Hanabi clapped excitedly. Perhaps encouraged by this, their father continued.

"So for Himawari, I suppose candy with…fresh cream would be better than anko or syrup candies. Cake or pudding or some such."

"I think that would be good. Really good. Right?" Hanabi cast a pointed look in Hinata's direction.

Hinata nodded firmly.

"Now that that's decided…" Their father started walking again at a vigorous pace that belied his years. "Once we get back to the village, I'll have to stop by the hamburger shop and the bakery!" He gradually pulled ahead of his daughters. He was moving so quickly, there was a chance he might break into a run.

"Honestly, Father. You get all worked up so quickly. I guess it's okay so long as you don't knock your back out again." Hanabi giggled. "Father? Do you need me to carry your things?"

Hanabi chased after their father, and Hinata watched as they grew smaller. He had changed. And he was trying to change again now. There was nothing in this world that didn't change.

The same could no doubt be said about me.

She had to change. From a pathetic mother who couldn't let her children go into one who properly acknowledged their growth.

"Hinataaaa! What are you doiiing?! We're leaving you!" Hanabi called.

Hinata gasped. Before she knew it, they had pulled far ahead of her.

She didn't have to worry about the house. Even if her husband didn't come home, Boruto was there. She could leave Himawari to him. So…maybe she could spend a little more time with these two, if they just needed someone to carry things. Hinata started to run.

2 MASTER SHINO! AND X CARDS!

The insects had finally calmed back down by the time Shino took a stroll down an alley in the old town. Far from the hustle and bustle, he enjoyed the warm light of the sun on his skin. He was *this* close to stretching out with abandon, regardless of what anyone thought.

However, when he did actually stretch out languidly, he stopped suddenly, like a puppet that had run out of chakra. His eyes grew round beneath his goggles, unable to fully take in the scene before him.

The master of the Hyuga main family was in front of the sweet shop, of all things. Hyuga Hiashi was the father of his former teammate, Hinata. Even to flatter them, he would have been hard-pressed to say that father and daughter were close; he'd never so much as seen them together. And he remembered how Hinata had seemed very unhappy every time the topic of her family came up. Thus, Shino had never exchanged so much as a word with Hiashi.

But the issue wasn't simply that he and Hinata didn't get along; it lay with Hiashi himself. He had a tendency to view

other clans as lesser somehow. Given that Shino belonged
to the Aburame clan, this kind of conversation tended to be
uncomfortable. But this was in the past now. He'd heard that
Hiashi had mellowed a great deal.

Shino walked over to him. "Hello!"

The older man slowly turned around. "Aren't you…
Aburame…"

"Shino, yes. I went out on missions on the same team as
your daughter."

"Oh. With Hinata." Hiashi grinned, broadly. The threat-
ening air that had once caused Shino to recoil was so dialed
down that Shino almost wondered if it had ever existed.

"What are you up to today in—" Shino glanced over to
check that the shop owner was too far away to hear him
before continuing. "In a place like this?"

The Hyugas were one of the leading families in Konohagakure—in other words, they were rich. Shino would have
thought they would go to the department store instead of a
sad little shop like this to buy sweets, to a place where they
carried the best luxury brands, half a dozen cookies all in
their own wrappers. Or else call a chef to their house and
have those sweets prepared for them.

"Hm?" Hiashi raised an eyebrow. "Just doing a little shopping."

Shino dropped his eyes. "Aah!" he said. "Extreme
Ninja, hm?"

X Cards. Shino knew about the game. He hadn't actually
bought any of the cards, but his students at the academy were
obsessed with them. He would sometimes hear their voices
inside when he was about to enter the classroom for a lesson.

"Shino festival!"

"Shino festival again!"

"Nah, seriously, it's a Shino festival!!"

By "Shino festival," the students meant that they kept getting Shino's card, which had the lowest rarity of C. It appeared so often it wasn't even a joke—it was a junk card. Every time he heard his students groaning at this, Shino was thankful for the goggles on his face. They kept anyone from noticing if a tear or two spilled from his eyes.

He was about to mention how surprising it was that Hiashi would be interested in Extreme Ninja. He'd simply assumed that this sort of commonplace dalliance was—

Krk, krk. He heard a faint, familiar sound. The sound of the Byakugan being activated.

Shino unconsciously dropped into a defensive posture and looked over at Hiashi to find that he was examining the X Card packs one after another with Byakugan eyes.

"This one's R. This one is, too. Mm, this is SSR. Ha ha! I found a good present for Boruto."

He couldn't possibly be...

He's looking inside the packs with his Byakugan and picking cards?! That's cheating...

In high spirits, Hiashi headed for the cash register, while behind him, Shino's shoulders slumped.

FATHER AND DAUGHTER, TABLE FOR ONE

"Judgement Day is coming." The man's voice echoed in the lightless room. "The people of Konoha lament that there is too little excitement nowadays. So then we would indeed be remiss if we did not offer them a little thrill, hm? Heh heh heh! Hee hee hee, ha ha ha!"

Other voices joined him in laughter.

"They will taste the Judgement of the Thunder God." The man grinned, but his smirk caught no one's eye in the murky darkness. "Let us distribute *this* throughout Konoha. We shall place it in the most prominent places to ensure as many as possible view our awesome proclamation. Heh heh heh heh!" The man waved his hand to show off the item he held in it.

However.

"It's too dark. We can't see it," a woman said.

"What? Ohh, I'm sorry." The man pulled out a lighter, and *bomf*—a small flame flickered to life, illuminating the pitch-black room with a red glow.

The woman who had spoken before now narrowed her eyes and carefully examined the large poster in the man's hand.

And then she groaned. "Come on. What is this? What's with the massive picture of a hamburger right in the middle there?"

"My newest burger," the man proclaimed with pride. "I call it 'Judgement of the Thunder God.' Very decisive, don't you think? I was going for something so powerfully spicy that it could satisfy all those people moaning about the lack of excitement lately. The second they bite into this bad boy, the shock to their tongue will be like a blow from the Thunder God—"

"That's not what I meant," the woman interrupted the man's matter-of-fact explanation of his new menu item and shook her head. "Why did you make it look like Thunder Burger's the main attraction? This poster's supposed to be for the annual Konoha Eating Contest. I'm sponsoring it, too, you know."

"As am I!"

"I'm in this, too!"

The other two shop owners joined her in voicing their complaints.

"I hear what you're saying." The owner of Thunder Burger shrugged, careful not to let his lighter go out. "But Ichiraku Ramen's right there at the bottom, on the left. Q's aged roast is in the center here. And Ankorodo's *zenzai* with rice flour dumplings is on the right, as you can see. Well, perhaps the images are a little *small*."

"Small is the problem!" the elderly owner of Ankorodo cried out, and the mistress of Yakiniku Q frowned next to her.

"At any rate, redo the poster." The woman—Ayame, second-generation owner of Ichiraku Ramen—sighed. "The four of us cosponsor this contest, so make all the photos the same size." She looked around the room. "And why is the Thunder Burger break room so dark? Did the light burn out or something?"

"No. I just replaced it the other day." The owner headed

toward the door and pressed the light switch. Instantly, a corner of the room was illuminated by an isolated, meager light.

Ayame arched an eyebrow. "That's hardly a light."

"I asked the part-timer to go get a lightbulb, and for some reason, he got this indirect light. It'd be a waste just to throw it out, so I decided to leave it for the time being." The man shrugged.

"Before, you talked about 'Judgement Day.' What was that supposed to mean?" the mistress of Yakiniku Q asked, leaving the matter of the lighting.

"It means I'll be the judge on that day since I'm the commentator and judge for the contest. I was trying to work myself up. I might not look it, but I'm actually nervous about doing this."

"Right." The mistress of Yakiniku Q slumped in her chair, wondering why she'd even bothered to ask.

"Should we get back to the topic at hand?" Ayame said. "So, the award to be presented to the winner. We've been taking turns, and this year…Ankorodo's up. I assume that's all right?"

"Mm-hmm." The elderly proprietress nodded. "I s'pose I could do an extra topping or some such. A free dumpling with your zenzai. Good until next year's eating contest. Perfect, hm?" She chuckled with satisfaction.

However.

"That's not enough." Thunder Burger put the brakes on. "We have to make this year stand out. After all, the Lord Seventh has decided the day will be a new holiday, Family Day. The prize has to be extravagant enough for such a special occasion. How about all the extra dumplings you can eat for a year?"

"That's—!" The elderly woman gasped. "That'll put me outta business! You can't have forgotten! *He* lives here in Konoha… Akimichi Choji!!"

Now everyone gasped. Silence. A quiet descended upon the room, as though they'd all been frozen in ice.

"So long as he's around, an all-you-can-eat's a no-go in this town. Isn't that right, Yakiniku?" The old woman turned to the owner of the yakiniku restaurant.

"True," she assented, her face pale. "I reserve the right to refuse all-you-can-eat to him alone."

"See what I mean? And yet here you are, talking about infinite extra dumplings, of all the foolishness." The elderly woman gritted her teeth. "I'll not be forgetting, I put up the prize in the contest four years ago... I got swept up in the excitement and decided on all-you-can-drink *amazake*. That man drank me right out of stock in a single day. I just barely stayed in business."

"But." The owner of Thunder Burger tried to placate the indignant woman. "If you do something extravagant, people will hear the name Ankorodo far and wide. This is a great opportunity. Customers might actually stay away if you only offer a prize of a single dumpling, you know?"

"Hngh!" Ankorodo's proprietress was speechless.

"Hell ahead, hell behind," Ayame said, taking pity on the elderly woman. "I suppose that's where we're at."

"If that's what you think, then we should—" the owner of Ankorodo started, furious, but her anger fizzled abruptly. "No, actually, that's good. That'll be the prize. As many extra dumplings in your zenzai as you want. Every dumpling in the universe if that's what it takes."

Ayame and the others exchanged a suspicious look, while the elderly woman lowered her face and continued quietly.

"I don't want to miss out on the advertising opportunity here, after all. It's a simple thing. And I've got my own secret strategy. You just wait and see. Hee hee hee hee..."

◎ ◎ ◎ ◎ ◎

"Bwah ha ha ha ha ha! Ha ha ha!" The bright laughter of
Akimichi Choji, the sixteenth head of the Akimichi clan,
rang out in the living room of the Akimichi residence. He was
lying on the sofa in front of the TV, stuffing potato chips in
his mouth. "Ha ha! Hee hee hee! Ha ha… Bwah!"

Chips spewed from his mouth, wide open in constant
laughter, and shot forward to cover the comic duo on the TV
in crumbs. Even that was funny.

"Haaa! Ha ha ha! Heh! Ha ha!" Choji slapped his stomach.
His plump belly made a satisfying sound—*boing boing*—and
as if in a joint performance, his backside cried, *Frrrt!* "Whoop-
sy. Guess I was hitting a little too hard. Ha ha ha ha ha!" He
exploded in laughter again, not learning anything from the
experience, ignorant of the scornful eyes piercing him from
behind.

"The worst," his daughter Cho-Cho groaned, eyes narrowed contemptuously. Her voice was cold, the icy edge of her
resentment at having to stand.

Next to her, Choji's wife, Karui, looked down on her
husband just as disdainfully. "You." She jerked her chin at
Cho-Cho. "Go get the illustrated animal encyclopedia from
the bookshelf. You know the one."

"What're you gonna do with an encyclopedia?" her daughter asked.

"Bring it down on your father's head with everything I
have."

Cho-Cho rolled her eyes. "Your jokes don't sound like jokes,
Mom. Maybe stop. Seriously."

"Well, then maybe I'll just flip through it. Might be something on how to take care of a useless, lazy old man."

"It won't. This kind of dad's only at our house."

The two women sighed in unison behind Choji and his merrily shaking belly.

"At any rate," Karui said. "Tidy up?"

"Right." Cho-Cho nodded.

Choji was surrounded by chip bags, all of them consommé flavor. The women gingerly stepped into the nest of the useless, lazy old man.

"Uh?" Karui questioned as she went around to the front of the sofa, eyes fixed on the floor. A non-chip bag lay empty there. "Hey, hon? Is this bag maybe…"

"Ha ha ha ha—Huh?" Choji stopped laughing, hearing the sudden weight in Karui's tone, in direct contrast to the "light" meaning of her name.

"I can't believe you." Karui looked up when she realized what the empty bag had once contained. "That was the sweet bread I bought for breakfast tomorrow! Why'd you go and eat it already?!"

"H-huh? Oh, you know." Choji shrugged. "I was getting bored of consommé, so I wanted something a little sweet—"

"Then eat a spoonful of sugar!!" she shouted fiercely, and shifted her gaze to another outrage. "And this! This milk! Why are you drinking it straight from the carton?! Can you not use a glass?! I've told you to stop doing this!!"

"It's fine, though. I mean, it's just us drinking it."

"That is *not* the point! Come on!" She grabbed his collar and tried to yank him up from the sofa. But given that he was about three times her size, although she moaned and groaned as she yanked and pulled—"Nnnngh! Dammit!"—Choji merely shifted from lying down to sitting up, and she was left gasping for air.

"W-whatever." She put her hands on her knees and panted.

"I'm tired from getting mad, and my arms are tired. I'm just tired all over."

While Karui was putting on this show of strength, Cho-Cho had collected the garbage on the floor, and she now fanned her sweating mother with an empty chip bag.

"Mom. I dunno. Forget it."

"Yeah." Karui waved a hand. "At any rate…I'm going to get groceries. I have to get…tomorrow's breakfast again…" She staggered toward the front door like she was still not getting enough oxygen.

"Oh! Shopping?" Choji called out happily behind her. "While you're at it, could you grab more consommé chips? We only have salt left."

Karui looked back over her shoulder, and a blood vessel popped up on her forehead. She silently turned away, stomped forward, and nearly yanked the front door off its hinges before slamming it shut with equal force. Even the living room shook from the impact, and the chip crumbs stuck to the TV peeled away and fluttered to the floor.

"W-what? Why's your mom so angry all of a sudden?" Choji plugged his ears against all the noise. But he could still hear Cho-Cho muttering for some reason.

"Useless, lazy old man."

Now that he had thoroughly tried his wife's patience, she was sure to leave him. He'd come to this realization by reflecting on his own behavior—no, there was none of that, of course. His daughter had informed him that he was in serious trouble.

That said, Choji had no idea what he could actually *do* about the situation. He boasted that he was the best in Konoha at the art of reading the doneness of fried meat, but even now, past the age of thirty, he still hadn't mastered the art of reading a woman's heart. Precisely because of this state of affairs, he couldn't come up with a way to win his wife back, no matter how he wracked his brain.

"At any rate, all this thinking's making me hungry," he declared. "Maybe I'll just go get some chips."

And that was the end of that.

"You've only been thinking for five minutes, though," Cho-Cho noted, with a wry smile. But she didn't try to talk him out of more chips. In fact, she decided to join him, and that's how he knew she was his daughter.

The day he'd taken over from his father as master of the Akimichi house, he'd given voice to the anxiety that had been plaguing him for as long as he could remember. Could a chubby guy like him *really* find someone to marry him?

That had been a needless worry. He managed to meet Karui, and they'd been blessed with this treasure of a child. He was aware that his was a charmed life. He just wasn't aware that he was a useless, lazy old man.

First of all, his daughter was adorable. It wasn't just the fond eye of a father talking; she was legitimately cute. Every night after she was born, he'd prayed by her bedside that she would take after Karui and not him, and his efforts had paid off. His wife had likened his form in prayer to "a craftsman watching over a ham to ensure it was smoked well," but that was fine— actually, no. It wasn't. Because of these wicked thoughts about ham getting mixed up with his prayers, his daughter's physique resembled a ham—that is to say, his own physique.

Still, she had her mother's face, so he couldn't complain. Those beautiful almond eyes. Her plump lips. *I'm just so glad my own genes are nowhere to be seen from the neck up*, Choji thought fondly, as he looked at her face.

"What? Why're you staring at me like that? Not my problem if you trip and fall," Cho-Cho said.

Choji gasped. There were a lot of people coming and going at the night market, and it was true that he might very well bump into someone if he didn't pull himself out of his own head.

"Dad, you bumped into a bunch of people while you were spacing out there, although they all just bounced off your stomach."

Or he had already bumped into someone. "I-it was their fault... Hey, I was just thinking...about how I can make up with your mom."

"Hmm. You come up with some brilliant idea?" she asked.

"No, nothing," he replied immediately.

Cho-Cho frowned, and Choji furrowed his brow, puzzled. "You gotta come up with one thing at least." She glared at him from the corner of her eye. "Even if it's some clichéd thing."

"Unnh... Like what?" He gave up right away.

"Think about it yourself for five seconds at least." She sighed heavily. "Sooo, liiiike, a present or something. What about a ring or jewelry?"

"Ohh." Choji pointed to his daughter's ears. "I gave you those earrings."

She pulled her lips into a tight line. "I'm not talking about stuff you've given *me*. I mean stuff you've given Mom."

The earrings Cho-Cho had been wearing were a present from his late master Asuma when Choji was promoted to chunin. The custom in the Nara, Yamanaka, and Akimichi clans was that the parent would give the earrings they themselves wore when their child became a genin until the child reached the chunin level and the earrings were returned.

Choji had originally given Cho-Cho the earrings when she was still attending the academy—before she'd made it to genin. He'd decided to give her the earrings early because she had already mastered a number of the Akimichi clan's traditional techniques. The Nara and Yamanaka clans had done the same.

But when it came to other presents he'd given...

"I don't think I've ever given your mom jewelry," he confessed.

"Whaaat?" Cho-Cho gaped at him.

"No. No, no. It's not like that." He waved his hands back and forth to excuse himself. "Your mom uses Lightning Style, right? So then, like, if she wears metal, she might end up getting a shock."

His daughter considered this for a moment. "You could just get her something leather."

"I guess so." He meekly accepted her rebuttal. He wasn't so self-absorbed that he thought he didn't have to try to keep Karui interested in him. But even when he did nothing, she stayed with him, and so he'd gradually convinced himself that this was the natural way of things. Except now that bill of sale was coming due.

"But, y'know, Mom's been with you all this time. So it's liiiike... I guess you got *something* going on, Dad," Cho-Cho concluded with a smile, but then quickly frowned. "Wow, awkward. I feel like I just said something super embarrassing. Forget it, just forget it." She covered her face with one hand and clawed at the air with the other.

Choji raised an eyebrow. Was what she said really that embarrassing?

"So, like, Dad." She peeked out from a gap in between her fingers. "What do you think you got to offer? Like, your strengths, the things about you Mom probably likes."

"What do I have to offer... That's a good question." He looked up at the night sky, as if digging around inside his head, looking for himself. One thing sprang to mind. "I'm pretty nice, I guess." An extremely innocuous self-evaluation.

"Whoa! So boring." Cho-Cho rolled her eyes in exasperation. And then abruptly opened them wide. A grin spread across her face. "If you have anything else to offer, Dad, it would be…" She snapped a finger out, pointing straight ahead. "The way you eat."

Choji followed his daughter's finger, which was pointed squarely at the twenty-four hour general store, his intended destination for the purposes of chip buying. She couldn't possibly be suggesting he buy everything in the store and devour all the snacks, could she? He quickly realized she wasn't pointing to the store itself, but at a poster pasted up to one side of the entrance.

"*Come together once again this year, gluttons of Konoha!*" it read. A notice for the annual eating contest. And there were pictures, too: a hamburger bright red with chili spices; ramen topped with a mountain of roasted pork that spilled over the edges of the bowl; yakiniku meat on the grill, sizzlingly juicy; creamy, sweet zenzai that made his mouth water.

"Oh ho." His stomach growled.

"All you have to do is enter the contest and show off the way you eat, Dad. And then Mom'll fall for you all over again." The solution to all problems was, in the end, eating. Like father, like daughter. "And look!" She moved her finger toward the bottom of the poster.

"*The contest will be held on Family Day this year, so participation is restricted to parent-child teams,*" it warned.

"So? You and me team up, we'll be a shoo-in for the grand prize." Cho-Cho pulled her finger back and popped her thumb up instead.

"Aah… Ah! Right!" Choji raised his own thumb back at her.

They turned to each other and grinned while their stomachs rumbled almost purposefully.

@ @ @ @ @

Family Day, the day of the big event. White smoke fluttered up into the cloudless blue sky. A large tent with a triangular roof had been set up on the athletic grounds in a corner of the old town, and seats were arranged in a tiered formation. The site had been specially prepared for the eating contest. Parents and children waited eagerly for the games to begin.

Catching sight of a face he knew, Choji waved cheerfully. "Shikamaru!"

"Hey, Choji." Nara Shikamaru raised a hand in return. At his side stood a boy with the exact same hair as his father, Nara Shikadai.

"Ugh," Shikadai grumbled when he noticed Cho-Cho and her father. "So you *are* here. That's...such a bother."

"Natch." Cho-Cho puffed out her chest. "You can count on me showing up wherever delicious food can be had, y'know?"

From his attitude, it seemed that Shikadai would really have preferred her not to be there. But she heard a different "ugh" from another direction. Turning around, she spotted Yamanaka Sai, who had married into the Yamanaka clan, and his son, Yamanaka Inojin.

Inojin's eyebrows were raised in an inverted V. "So Uncle Choji's in the contest and not Auntie Karui? We'll never win. Not like this."

Sai gave him a wry smile. "Well, won't know until we try, right?" That said, Sai wasn't particularly optimistic himself.

"So Ino's holding the fort down at home?" Choji asked.

"The flower shop's busy because of the holiday, too," Sai explained. "I could've watched the shop, but..."

"If it's busy, then all the more reason to leave it to her," Shikamaru interjected.

"Right, exactly," Choji agreed. "She's been working in that shop since she was a kid. She'll have things under control, no matter how busy it gets in there."

"I guess so." Sai smiled with relief—and looked sad somehow. This was always the face he made when a member of Ina-Shika-Cho talked about when they were kids. He hadn't been a part of their lives back then.

If even Choji had picked up on this, then naturally, Shikamaru had, too. He jabbed a sharp elbow into Choji's side, and the larger man hurriedly opened his mouth to apologize. But then he heard another "ugh" from yet another direction.

"I-I'm so nervous." A boy with hair in a bowl cut looked as green as the jumpsuit he wore. "I'm going to puke. Ugh… Urp."

"Calm down, Metal! Calm—no! Actually, it would be better to throw up! Throw up and empty out your stomach!" Next to him, a similarly bowl-cutted man in a green jumpsuit (although the arms were ripped off at the shoulders) yelled encouragement—or something along those lines—at the boy. "Throoow up! Throoow up!"

Metal Lee and Rock Lee.

Choji stared, preferring if possible not to witness any gross scenes before he started eating, and the father Rock gave a thumbs-up and a big smile.

"No need to worry! We had fruits and vegetables of all colors of the rainbow for breakfast this morning. I've no doubt that my son's vomit will be a beautiful rainbow as well!"

No one wanted that kind of beauty, nor did anyone want to hear about it, but Rock made the declaration anyway, full of confidence.

"Umm." Choji opened his mouth to change the topic to anything else. "So who all is coming then? I guess Naruto's not here?" He glanced around.

"Not likely." Shikamaru shook his head. "He insisted

he could finish up on his own. He was trying to give me a break, but I know there was so much work left, he'd have to go straight through till morning." He clucked his tongue in irritation.

It didn't seem like they'd get anywhere good following that path, so Choji grasped for another topic of conversation. "Th-that reminds me. It's strange to see you and Sai here. I mean, at an eating contest. I guess the prize was just too tempting?"

"Yeah." Shikamaru nodded. "Temari pestered me about it. Endless zenzai dumplings at Ankorodo. The dumplings are just supposed to be a bonus, though. The azuki beans are the core of zenzai. Who needs so many dumplings anyway?"

"'Pestering' makes it sound cute, but it was anything but. I mean, yesterday, Mom—" Shikadai grumbled and then shuddered at the memory of it.

"Sounds like what happened to us," said Sai.

"An eating contest is an event of youth! You can't miss it!" shouted Rock Lee.

"And what about you, Choji? Oh, I guess I don't have to ask." Shikamaru narrowed his eyes in laughter.

"Nah, we—" Choji started and then hesitated. He couldn't actually say he was there to show off for his wife about what a great eater he was, so he scrambled for a different excuse.

"Ha ha ha ha ha!" A throaty laugh echoed across the grounds. It was a voice he'd never heard before.

Sai looked back, puzzled. Following his lead, a little ways off, Choji noticed a giant who could have been mistaken for one of the Akimichi clan. And another one. The first was a tall, hefty man, torso naked to reveal his muscular body. The other didn't quite match up in terms of height, but what he lacked in height he made up for in girth. He was also not wearing a shirt, and his protruding belly hung over the top of his pants, jiggling like white *mochi* rice cakes. Both had their arms crossed and were bent forward toward each other.

"You lot have such weak reasons for being here!" the muscular one shouted.

"There is food to eat here, and so we eat!" the fat one continued. "That's all a glutton needs!"

"Haven't seen you around before. So who are you guys?" Shikamaru asked.

The muscular one laughed, his trapezius muscles twitching. "We are wandering gluttons, father and son! We came this year, lured in by the delicious scent! I'm the cleaner of the bottom of pots, Kui!"

"And his son!" the fat one followed. "Pecking at stacked lunch boxes, Daore!"

They sent each other a signal with their eyes and then shouted in unison, "Together we are—"

"*Kuidaore*—Eat till You Drop," Cho-Cho muttered, and the massive father and son froze.

A quiet wind blew past in the not-so-brief silence that followed.

"Hey, read the room," Shikadai murmured with annoyance, his mouth up against Cho-Cho's ear. "You coulda just let them say it. I mean, come on."

Father and son trembled with a barely repressed desire to continue before bellowing out, "Together we are *Daorekui*— Drop till You Eat!"

"Wow, yikes. You just flipped it around." Inojin frowned.

"And it doesn't even make sense when you put your names together backwards!" Metal Lee snapped out a finger. "It's meaningless!"

"Details!" shouted Kui or Daore—or maybe both of them. At any rate, there was shouting.

"You with your hierarchy of small builds and small appetites. Small, small! You're small, too!" Kui pointed at Shikamaru, Sai, and Rock Lee in turn. He turned to Choji and then stopped. "You—I guess it won't do to call you small. You're about the only one who comes close to matching my powerful stomach. Isn't that right, Akimichi Choji?"

Choji furrowed his brow. It seemed that this father-son team knew him, but he had no memory of the stern man before him.

"Impossible." Kui's massive bulk staggered backwards. "You mean to say you have forgotten our names?! Last year! And the year before! And the year before that!! We are comrades in gluttony! We have challenged each other to our caloric limits!"

"I hear you." Choji shrugged. "But when I'm eating, all I see is the food."

Shikamaru and the others were merely perplexed, but Kui took this excuse as a grave personal affront.

"Yooouuuuu... How shameless!" His face went beet red in the blink of an eye. "Acting so high and mighty... I'll have you in tears later! When it comes to gluttony, this father and son cannot be beat! Kuidaore! Eat till You Drop!!" Kui and Daore walked away, laughing loudly.

Everyone there gaped at this barrage of declarations.

"I *knew* it was Eat till You Drop," Cho-Cho muttered, and then they heard a voice announcing the start of the contest.

◎　◎　◎　◎　◎

"Thank you so much for taking time out of your busy schedules to join us for the Konoha Eating Contest today. We're happy to have you all here with us..."

Sitting at the front of the grounds, Choji sent his eyes racing across the crowd before him as he listened absently to the owner of Thunder Burger up on the stage.

"Oh! Dad, over there. Looks like she came." Cho-Cho pointed into the audience from her seat next to him.

And there she was: his wife, Karui. She looked terribly bored, resting her chin in one hand, but she had come to watch them at least.

"All right. All that's left now is to chow down." He hit his stomach like a drum before setting his fists on the table—the *where's the grub?* pose, to put it crudely.

Their table was a simple two-person affair. Similar tables were set out at regular intervals, about a hundred altogether, which meant that nearly a hundred pairs of parents and children were taking part in the contest. To their left was Eat till You Drop. To their right were Shikamaru and Shikadai. Next to them were Sai and Inojin. And further beyond them still were the Lees. He was surrounded by familiar faces, perhaps because they had all signed up for the contest one after the other.

"Now then, getting right to it, allow me to introduce today's first meal. From Ichiraku Ramen, specially prepared for the contest, pork ramen with extra thick slices of roasted pork!"

A pushcart loaded with ramen was brought in, and a cry of appreciation rose up from the crowd.

"Th-this is—!" Choji groaned, powerfully moved.

The familiar Ichiraku bowl was covered in thick pork slices, so many that they nearly spilled over the edges. It wasn't just a flat layer that covered the top of the bowl, however; the slices were piled up toward the center, peaked in a pork mountain. Rather than being roughly tossed on, the meat was arranged in a neat spiral that grew steepr as it neared the summit. When Choji saw the tidy bit of *naruto* wakame seaweed on top of this mountain, he assumed it was meant as a tip of the hat to the Lord Seventh. Under the blue sky, the translucent drops of fat on the surface reflected the bright sunlight, and Choji and Cho-Cho's faces shone with great delight.

"Our eaters will compete to finish this limited edition ramen the fastest! Only the top thirty pairs will be able to go on to taste our next dish! Now, let's welcome the cameras from the studio broadcasting today's events. Everyone in the village will be watching the contest play out, so please make sure you put on your best faces, all right, eaters? Remember—if you vomit, you will be immediately disqualified!"

The abrupt appearance of the word *vomit* gave Choji a bad feeling, and he glanced over at the Lee table.

"B-but I'm just not feeling well. And now this…this huge bowl…in front of me…" Eyes darting from side to side, Metal Lee pressed a hand to his mouth, flustered.

Choji immediately averted his eyes, and so was not a witness to what followed.

"W-w-what is going on here?! Lee is splaaaaaashing out! Before the eating's even begun?! What is happening?! Ah, but this is some rainbow! The many colors of this mess splashing in an arc is just like a rainbooooow! Yes. Well, then, the Lee family is disqualified!"

"Metal, don't worry about it! Vomiting is just a part of youth! I mean, your old dad here's thrown up doing push-ups, I've thrown up doing headstands… At any rate, I've done a lot of barfing!"

Thanks to the commentary from both the burger shop owner and Rock Lee, however, Choji got the general idea.

Although the Ichiraku pork ramen was extremely satisfying, the dish that followed—the powerfully spicy Judgement of the Thunder God hamburger—was quite a difficult foe. Choji managed somehow to withstand the terrible "heated excitement" and finish the burger, groaning all the while, to advance to the semi-finals with Shikamaru and Sai. Now he cooled his swollen lips with an ice pack in one of the break tents, while Cho-Cho quietly sipped water.

"Aah," he moaned. "That was a close one."

"You said it. I'd rather squeeze a whole tube of wasabi directly onto my tongue than eat that again."

"What are you two doing?" A visitor, Karui.

"Mom!" Cho-Cho cried.

Forgetting about his swollen lips, Choji stood up. "You came to see me in action! The way I'm eating, you can't help but fall in love all over again, right?"

"I'm here, too, you know," his daughter interjected pointedly. "It's *us. We*."

"Yeah, yeah. *Us* in action!" Choji puffed his chest out.

"Action… Well, that's one way of putting it." Karui's reaction was lukewarm compared to what he'd expected. "An eating contest's basically a gathering of fools, though. Are you competing on food and speed, or are you competing to see who can wreck their body the fastest? To call it *action* is a bit much."

"M-much?" Choji parroted the word back at her.

"I mean, feeding you that greasy stuff… Is the funeral home actually behind this thing? I didn't see any ads for them. Well, don't go overboard in your foolishness. And make sure you get some vegetables in there, too." Karui waved a hand and then left the tent.

The father-daughter duo gaped after her.

"So the way you eat…*isn't* what she loves," Cho-Cho muttered, blinking rapidly.

"Now then, here we are at the semi-finals at last! Our eaters will be enjoying…"

Klakka klakka. Sitting on the pushcart was a tabletop gas range with an iron grill, a side dish of lettuce, and steaming meat, already cooked.

"Aged roast for ten from Yakiniku Q! The first three teams to completely finish this hearty helping will advance to the finals. Aaaaand! What is wrong, Akimichis?! Dad's gone totally limp!!" The owner of Thunder Burger shouted as Choji slumped in his seat and stared into space with dead eyes.

"What exactly…*does* she love…?" The dazed words melted into the blue sky.

"Hey, Dad! Get it together! The next dish is here, all right?!" Cho-Cho shook him violently. Choji merely allowed his massive bulk to sway from side to side.

"I don't know what's going on…but this tasty treat waits for no one! Let's get started on the semi-final round!"

"Hmph!" Kui snorted loudly at the next table. "How pedestrian. To balk at that tiny plate, to collapse under the pressure of carbohydrates. You're nothing but a small man, after all. My greatest shame in life is that I ever considered you a rival."

"Choji," Shikamaru murmured, worried.

However.

"All right then. Semi-finals…staaaaart!"

Bong! The gong sounded before Shikamaru's concern had a chance to reach Choji, who had clearly lost the will to fight.

"Gaah! Fine!" Cho-Cho turned from her father to face the steaming plate in front of her. She raised her chopsticks, gathered up several pieces of meat, and brought them to her mouth. "So good! Dad, this meat is totally delicious!"

Her smile glistened with meat juice, but Choji remained slumped in dejection. Normally, he would drool copiously at the mere mention of delicious meat, but now his mouth simply hung open slovenly.

"No reaction to meat, either? This is serious!" Sweat springing up on her brow, Cho-Cho kept moving her chopsticks. "And there's so much here. I mean, sure, it's *good*, but me polishing it off all by myself's kinda..." For once in her life, she was actually intimidated by food. The meat had been piled high to be shared by parent and child, and even she hesitated in the face of such a challenge.

"Whoops-y! Three minutes in, and already someone's cleaned their plate!"

"What?! Seriously? Already?!" Cho-Cho looked around and locked eyes with Kui, who was picking at his teeth with a toothpick. He flashed her a grin and made a show of having room to spare with a flourish of his fingers—or rather, his toothpick. But it hadn't been an easy meal. His son Daore was slumped over just like Choji.

And they weren't the only ones who were finished.

"I seriously...never want to eat meat again," Shikadai groaned.

"Don't talk like that. You'll be missing rice and meat in a week," Shikamaru replied. "Although I *definitely* won't be."

The plate before this pair was also empty. Father and son looked about ready to fall off their chairs.

"Dad," Inojin sighed. "You can have the rest." He and Sai were very nearly done, too, only a few pieces of meat left before them.

"No need to hold back," Sai protested, weakly. "You're still a growing child."

"None of that matters. For real... This fatty meat's too much..." Both son and father were limp with exhaustion, and neither reached out for the remaining pieces of meat.

"Only one more team can advance to the finals! Which family will come out on top?!"

"Hngh… Hey, Dad! Snap out of it already! Come on!" Cho-Cho slapped her father's stomach.

But Choji didn't so much as look at his chopsticks. "My…appeal…"

Gritting her teeth, Cho-Cho suddenly picked up several pieces of lettuce in a flash on insight and quickly wrapped them around the remaining meat. "Dad, look at this! Vej! Tah! Bulz!"

"What…?" A spark flickered in his dead eyes.

"Mom said you should eat your vegetables, right?" she said. "Don't you think she'll fall in love all over again if she sees you eating vegetables?"

"This…is a vegetable?" Despite the fact that the meat was clearly spilling out from the lettuce.

"Vej! Tah! Bulz!" Cho-Cho kept at it.

"Right… Vegetable… Vegetablessss!" Choji sprang forward. In a single breath, he polished off this lettuce-meat. Next to him, Cho-Cho secretly struck a triumphant pose.

They heard the sound of the gong just as he stuffed the rest of the lettuce into his mouth. "And semi-finals are oooooover! Moving onto the finals are Eat till You Drop, the Naras, and the Akimichis! They managed to claw their way to the top in this fierce battle, so how about we all give them a big round of applause!"

As the audience's applause rang out through the grounds, they also heard the *thunk* of Sai and Inojin falling prostrate on their table, unable to finish the last of their meat.

"Now then, let's get straight to the final round! For your eating pleasure, the last dish of the day iiiiiis…zenzai with dumplings for ten from Ankorodo!"

The pushcart appeared once more, and the tabletop grills

were cleared away. In their place, ten bowls of zenzai appeared.

"So no break? Ugh. I don't really want to put anything more in my stomach," Shikadai grumbled with a sour face.

The look on Shikamaru's face was much the same, but he still managed to produce a slight smile. "It's like your mom always says, right? We've got a separate stomach for sweets. All we can do now is believe in her and cram this in it. Okay? You got space in there, yeah?" He poked his son in the side.

"Oh! Urp! Dad, stop it." Shikadai turned green. "Everything I ate's gonna come right back out!"

"Tsk tsk tsk!" The very first to react was the owner of Thunder Burger, gripping the microphone. "Vomiting is not allowed! No vomiting! Let's hurry up and get started!" He raised his arm up high.

"The final round of the Konoha eating contest starts... nooooooooow!"

His arm sliced downward through the air at the same moment the gong sounded.

"Daaad...I can't..." The younger member of Eat till You Drop abruptly passed out.

"Tch!" Kui clicked his tongue. "Pathetic. Throwing in the towel over something like this." Not only was he not worried for his son, he was actively scornful.

"Hey." Cho-Cho pursed her lips and frowned at him. "You don't gotta talk like that, do you?"

"You would have me sympathize with a loser? He might be my own son, but those with small appetites have no right to sit at the dinner table. In the end, supper is something we taste in solitude. The sole contributor to my victory is my stomach!" Kui began to shovel zenzai into his mouth.

"I got a bad feeling about this. Well, if he's eating all by himself, then he's no match for us. Right?" Cho-Cho patted her father's shoulder.

"Th-the vegetables are sticking to my throat... I can't... breathe..." Daore wasn't alone now; Choji also tipped over backward, chair and all.

"Huh?! Dad?!" Cho-Cho shouted.

"Choji!" Shikamaru cried.

"Mwah ha ha ha!" Kui laughed loudly enough to drown out both of them and started to trash talk his opponent, firmly convinced of his own victory. "It looks like your time is over, Choji. Be a good boy then and have a meal that's more your speed—"

His mouth stopped moving, abruptly.

"Your speed—your—bworf..."

Suddenly, something white and springy flew out of Kui's mouth.

◎ ◎ ◎ ◎ ◎

"Hee hee hee hee." Behind the personnel tent, the elderly owner of Ankorodo snickered to herself. "That's what you get."

She twisted her fingers together in a complicated fashion, weaving mysterious signs.

"Don't go underestimating me. I might be nothing more than an old lady running a sweets shop now, but back in my day, I was a ninja of incredible skill. People called me Sweets Princess... Although, actually, no one ever really called me that." Her voice was hollow. "Anyway! I used a special sugar for those dumplings, super enlarged with my Earth Style. I wanted to crush that darned Akimichi Choji. I never dreamed he'd destroy himself before I could get to him. I s'pose it's fine. I don't care who's in the lead, no way I'm giving anyone that prize. If the dumplings get too big, no one can finish the zenzai and I win either way!"

The elderly proprietress laughed gleefully, then stopped abruptly.

"Aah, hold on a sec. It's been a long time since I used Earth Style... How do you stop the enlargement again?"

◎　◎　◎　◎　◎

Countless dumplings spilled over from thirty trays and quickly grew so large in size that people had to crane their necks
to look up at them. The sweet treats destroyed not only the
tables and tent, but threatened to swallow up the audience.

"Konoha Hurricane!" Metal Lee launched a roundhouse
kick at an enormous dumpling closing in on a mother
and daughter.

"Konoha Great Hurricane!!" Rock Lee shot a dropkick
toward the center of the grounds.

However.

"Hngh! It's so chewy and springy, we just bounce back,"
father groaned to son. "There's no end to it!"

Meanwhile, elsewhere.

"Ninja Art of Beast Mimicry!"

A pack of large ink lions and smaller colorful lions charged
the dumplings. Although they just barely managed to stop
the terrible rice flour pushing forward, the majority of the
lions were crushed under the dumplings and disappeared on
the spot.

"Dad, is your brush weaker than usual?" Inojin asked.

"Maybe I just ate a little too much," Sai replied. "Inojin, on
your left!"

"Got it!"

Opposite where Sai and Inojin were battling fiercely to keep
the dumplings from escaping the field, a shadow slithered
along the ground.

"Kagemane Shadow Possession Technique!"

Although Shikadai's shadow checked the dumplings'
movement, it did nothing to stop them from swelling to larger
and larger sizes, and he frowned as he stepped back. "Such a
bother. Dad, you got any good ideas?!"

"I'm thinking." Shikamaru's own shadow was split into several branches, the tips piercing the dumplings like skewers. "This'll stop 'em. But there are too many. This really is a bother." He clicked his tongue.

In front of the podium, Cho-Cho was pushing dumplings back with two massive hands. "It's supposed to be food, and here it is trying to eat me. Get back to being sticky rice and try again!" She braced herself with a cry, but the dumplings were too chewy, and instead of moving out of the way, they actually swallowed up her hands, jiggling all the while.

"Huh?! What the—No way!" Her eyes grew wide. Then a dazzling bolt of lightning jetted down and shocked the dumpling, crackling. The world in front of her flickered from the shock, but once that died down, the dumpling had hardened and she was able to pull her hands away.

"What are you doing? Honestly." Karui landed beside her, having leapt down from the spectator seats.

"Mom!"

"I guessed there's Earth Style involved here, and look, just like I figured. Leave it to Lightning Style now." Karui flexed her bicep, but then quickly looked around. "By the way, where's your dad?"

"He's…" Cho-Cho started, but then froze in place. "Where *is* he anyway?"

His nostrils opening involuntarily, Choji took in the delicious scent of fat together with the aroma of sesame oil and burned garlic. He could hardly stand it: the fragrant scent of yaki-niku, one he never tired of no matter how many times he smelled it.

He opened his closed eyes slightly, and a familiar table at Yakiniku Q came into view. Just as he'd imagined, several pieces of meat were laid out on the grill in the center, fat bubbling up on them. And then he saw there was someone sitting on the other side of the table.

"Master Asuma?" He hadn't intended to say the name; it just slipped out. Maybe because that was where his master usually sat, and maybe because it *felt* like his master there.

However.

"What are you talking about, Choji?"

It was not his late master.

"Dad..."

It was the previous head of the Akimichi clan, Akimichi Choza.

"Hmph! They're almost done. Just fried enough." His father calmly shifted the nicely browned meat onto a small plate.

Choji gaped at this smooth movement. "Dad. I...have a family, too."

His father snorted in laughter, as if to ask why he was stating the obvious.

He dropped his gaze to the burnt bits of meat on the grill. "There's so much I wanted to talk to you about, Dad, if I got to see you again. About Karui, about Cho-Cho. I was just part of an eating contest with her until a minute ago... I can't remember why I'm here now."

Eyes closed, his father quietly ferried meat to his mouth with his chopsticks. Choji didn't know whether the smile that spread across his face was because he was satisfied with the flavor or because of him.

"Dad," Choji said, through gritted teeth. "You got any idea...what my appeal is?"

His father finished the last bite and set his chopsticks down firmly before narrowing his eyes to look squarely at him. "You're nicer than anyone else."

"Cho-Cho said that was just average, though."

"And what's so bad about average? Plenty of people out there don't have a single point in their favor, you know." His father laughed out loud. "When you were a child, Asuma always told you to be more confident." He put some money on the table for the meal and got to his feet, looking pained. His father was about to leave, just like that. Somewhere, forever.

"Dad? Wait! I still have so much I want to—"

His father looked down on him, baffled. "I am still alive, yes?"

Choji blinked rapidly. "Uh-huh. I know. But I never manage to make it back home, so it's like I have so much I want to say when we meet… What's with that, all of a sudden?"

"Oh, just a feeling. It really is just a feeling, but…you're talking as though to someone you haven't seen in a while. I am still alive, yes?" his father asked for the second time. "I know a thing about eating contests. Truth is, I wanted to take part myself. Pair up with my son. Father and son, you know?" His father pointed toward him and smiled with satisfaction.

"Instead, I'm consoling myself by walking around eating the same dishes as you are in the contest. Next is Ichiraku Ramen. They're serving something like the contest ramen. And then I'm going to have the Judgement of the Thunder God at Thunder Burger."

"I think you should pass on the Judgement of the Thunder God," Choji advised.

"Really?" His father raised an eyebrow. "Well, it is dull to eat alone. Food really needs to be shared."

"But you polished off the yakiniku by yourself," Choji protested.

"That's not what I meant." Choza chuckled.

Choji was baffled. He couldn't understand what his father

meant. "Oh!" he cried all of a sudden. He thought he finally understood why Karui had been so angry a few days earlier.

"Well, pop by the house once things settle down. It'll make your mother happy. We'd like to have a meal with our grand-daughter, too."

Choji bobbed his head up and down. His father also nod-ded, seemingly satisfied, and started to head for the door.

"Oh! Also." He turned around, as if remembering some-thing. "Your strength isn't only that you're so nice. I think you realized it yourself a long time ago, but...looks like you've forgotten. Baffling, really. You..."

Maybe it was his life flashing before his eyes. A vision on the verge of death. Or just a dream.

At any rate, Akimichi Choji was no longer lost.

@ @ @ @ @

"W-w-what are we gonna do?! Dad might still be in there!" Cho-Cho waved toward the dense zone of massive dumplings crowded together in close formation.

Karui clicked her tongue. "I *told* him that he needed to keep his idiocy in check... I'm not interested in being a widow!" She was about to charge in without any plan whatsoever.

Then the center of the dumplings pack puffed up, and an enormous figure shot out like lava from an erupting volca-no—first a head, followed by shoulders, chest, and then a massive body.

"Is that...Dad?!" Cho-Cho cried.

The size of a skyscraper, Choji spread his legs apart, ready to support his own weight. His floating feet touched the ground. The earth shuddered, and the dumplings coiling about his body fell away like droplets of water.

He glared down at the area and then immediately ripped a dumpling up from the ground and stuffed it into his mouth. And then another, and still one more. The herd of dumplings that threatened to bury the grounds steadily disappeared into his stomach.

"Don't go overboard, Choji!" came Shikamaru's shout from somewhere. "We don't know how much they'll expand! Your stomach'll split in half!"

And true to this warning, Choji's stomach started to churn after he'd eaten all the dumplings. Cho-Cho held her breath.

But in the next instant.

"Eating all by yourself…"

Fwp! Butterfly wings the color of the sky spread out.

"Sorryyyyyyyy!!" Choji's cry echoed through the area. As the wings sucked calories from him, his flabby body firmed up. Thanks to the vast calorie expenditure of this technique, the dumplings in his stomach had been entirely consumed by the time the changes in his physical body settled down.

"All by yourself…?" Cho-Cho looked up, bathed in the pale blue sunlight filtered through his massive wings. "You mean the dumplings? You're about the only one who could eat all that."

"I don't think that's quite what he means." Karui chuckled quietly, as if she alone understood the situation.

◎ ◎ ◎ ◎ ◎

"The winner of this year's eating contest is…the Akimichi familyyyyyyy!"

Firecrackers popped, and confetti rained down on the awards podium. Cho-Cho and a now-slender Choji lowered their heads with embarrassed smiles.

"If that'd kept up a second more, we would've had a serious disaster on our hands. And yet the contest kept going!" Inojin muttered, dumbfounded, as he stood behind the awards podium.

"A bunch of stuff got broken, but no one was hurt. So it's all good. And they nabbed the old lady behind it all, too." Shikadai clasped his hands behind his head.

Beside him, Metal Lee bobbed his head up and down. "Your dad's pretty scary when he's mad, huh?"

"Well, no wonder after getting lectured by that old woman," Shikadai replied. "After all, there's a little thing called position. Being a grown-up's all kinds of hassle."

Shikamaru shrugged, and Sai offered a wry smile.

"Normally, this should be reported to the police, though. I think a little punishment from them would be good, too."

Snap! Rock Lee thrust forward the palm of his hand. "No. There's no need to go that far. The owner of Ankorodo will be more than sufficiently punished."

"Mm. Unlimited dumpling zenzai," Sai noted. "It's simply exquisite given that she's up against the stomach of *the* Akimichi Choji."

"Quite sophisticated taking both the winner into consideration and doling out punishment to Ankorodo at the same time," Daore added, and the Eat till You Drop father-son duo guffawed loudly, while everyone else stared at them, wondering what they were even doing there.

"Mom, they're gonna take a commemorative photo. You're here anyway, how about you be in it, too?" Cho-Cho called out to Karui from the awards podium.

"What? Me? Why? I didn't do anything," Karui protested, even as she started to walk over.

"You're my mom. You don't need any other reason."

"Right, exactly," Choji agreed. "And you're my wife. That's plenty of reason."

Karui cocked her head to one side, persuaded by their arguments, or perhaps not. With no further objections, she stood next to Cho-Cho.

"So what do you wanna do after this? Should we go for unlimited dumplings straight away?" Cho-Cho grinned.

"We were almost crushed by dumplings just now... People are usually traumatized by that sort of thing, you know. To the point where they'd never want to even see a dumpling again. And yet you're already talking about eating them. Amazing..." Karui was impressed, but the look on Choji's face was complicated.

"You ate too many, huh, Dad? Well, I guess. If you're gonna chow down like that." Cho-Cho nodded.

"Hm? Oh, no, no, it's not that." Choji touched a hand to his perfectly flat stomach. "I just had some sweets, so I wanted to get a different flavor in there. How about we pick up some consommé chips and then head over?"

"So you're actually going to keep eating?!" Karui shouted.

Snap! The camera captured the moment. A laughing family in the frame, far removed from any notion of having exhausted love or patience.

3 MASTER SHINO! AND FAMILY!

He could enjoy Family Day all by himself. Actually, in fact, it was because he was alone that he could enjoy it. Shino clutched a paper bag as he walked through the throngs of people. Limited edition *oyakodon* chicken-and-egg rice bowl—parent and child, as it were—for Family Day. Twice the usual bowl size, it was apparently intended to be eaten by parent and child together. But if you were alone, you could have that extra portion all to yourself.

He'd been strolling along, buying food and eating it since the morning, so his stomach was already full to bursting. But he'd just gone ahead and bought the oyakodon when he came across it at a food stall. He'd gotten caught up in the festive mood again.

Forget breakfast the next morning; he was sure this would end up tucked away for his lunch the next day. But still Shino's heart was sufficiently buoyed by the sense that he'd gotten a great deal.

How long's it been since I got all worked up about food?

He was practically Akimichi Choji here.

"Aah, I'm starving."

He heard the voice of Choji himself.

"Here we go!"

And the voice of his former student Cho-Cho.

They were standing in front of the old-fashioned sweets shop, Ankorodo. He didn't know what exactly had happened, but Choji was slim for the first time in a while.

"What took you so long?" Choji's wife, Karui, was sitting at a table in front of the shop. "I thought you'd be here right away. Did you *really* go and get chips?" She pushed the bowls on the table toward Choji and Cho-Cho.

"Whoa, this looks so gooood!" Cho-Cho cried with delight.

"The absolute best thing after chips is something sweet to finish off!" Choji was no less delighted as he looked down at the contents of his bowl: zenzai with smooth white dumplings bobbing in it.

"The two of you can really eat," Karui sighed. "I get full just watching you."

"Dad devoured those dumplings, but I haven't had any zenzai yet," Cho-Cho noted. "If you're not eating yours, Mom, can I have them?"

"No, I'm going to eat them." Karui gave them a wry smile.

Shino watched over this scene, charmed. Karui was one of Cho-Cho's guardians, but because Choji took the lead when it came to their daughter, he'd never had the chance to speak to her. All Shino knew about Karui were strange rumors, like she had gone one-on-one with Naruto before he became Hokage and beaten him black and blue, and without getting a scratch.

Whatever the truth of it, she was right there, so he figured he should at least go say hello. But when he was about to approach the table, he realized it wasn't just the sweet scent of zenzai wafting over from the table.

Choji had his mouth full of dumplings. Cho-Cho was pinching the little white clouds from her mother's bowl. And Karui, annoyed by this, was stealing her daughter's zenzai itself.

The fun they were having was reaching him, loud and clear. Shino stopped. He didn't want to intrude on this happy family. At the same time, he suddenly realized Family Day wasn't something to be enjoyed alone. What *they* were doing over there was the real way to spend Family Day.

Family… No. Shino dropped his gaze to the bag in his hand. *Parent and child, hm?*

A large oyakodon bowl for parent and child. An amount he could never finish all on his own.

"Maybe I'll head over to see my dad." Shino turned around and started to walk toward his parents' home.

FATHER AND DAUGHTER, COLD FLAMES AND ROILING FIRE

The village of Konohagakure had changed remarkably. In the midst of the endless stream of people coming and going, Uchiha Sasuke acknowledged that it was a difficult task to try and remember the way it used to look. And it was easy for him to find a reason for that. The times had changed. The town was different. He'd been away for too long. He could list off any number of "official" reasons.

But in reality, although he'd spent his boyhood in the village, had he *ever* paid attention to any of it? When he was little, he was always looking at the back of his older brother, Uchiha Itachi, no matter where his eyes turned. After Itachi left the village, everything Sasuke saw reminded him of his brother: the signs in the park were his brother's words; the clusters of trees in town, his brother's form; the shadow reflected in the surface of the lake, his brother's face; the spots on the wall, his brother's gaze.

He'd never paid attention to any of the sights in town. He'd only looked through them and seen Itachi. It was no wonder then that he couldn't remember it. Without knowing

Itachi's true intentions, Sasuke had been held a prisoner of vengeance. There was no reason he should be able feel any nostalgia now.

Wait. Sasuke quickly pushed back against his own thoughts. He smelled something familiar on the wind: the fragrant aroma of fresh wood. He sniffed the air again and remembered that this was the scent of the material used for the walls in the Uchiha home. It brought to mind a memory of when his parents were still alive.

His mother standing in the kitchen. His father at the low table, arms crossed, eyes closed. And his own young self, looking at his father anxiously.

I guess I have some nostalgia left in me after all. The thought was mostly self-depreciating. He wasn't the only one who had watched Itachi. His father had also only ever seen him. Once upon a time, Sasuke must have been desperate for his father to look at *him*.

In the old memory, the child, traces of baby fat still lingering, opened his mouth to try and get his father's attention. *"Father… Where is the house?"*

Where is the house? He took a moment to reflect on the question, but it remained opaque. Had he really asked something like that?

No, he answered himself, immediately. *That's the question I'm asking myself now*.

"Where's the house?" Sasuke muttered to himself, interrupting his journey down memory lane. He had intended to make his way to the house where his wife and daughter lived now that he was back in his home village after a lengthy time away, but for some reason, there was nothing but an empty lot before his eyes. Building materials were piled high in one corner, the apparent source of the wood he'd smelled earlier.

But there was no house.

He pulled a tattered scrap of paper from his pocket. An address had been scribbled on the reply to a mission notification from a few years earlier, along with the message that his wife Sakura had built a house. He checked it one more time, but no, this was definitely the place.

And yet there was no house.

As he considered the likely causes of this situation, he struck upon a single possibility: genjutsu. Perhaps done simply as a bad joke, or maybe something more clearly malicious. He had no idea whose work it could be. There were simply too many possibilities. He'd earned the enmity of countless idiot thugs. On top of that, any number of people had their sights set on the Rinnegan in his left eye. This was also one of the reasons he couldn't come home to Konoha too often. But none of those people would have hidden the house with genjutsu, would they?

Sasuke shook his head. He didn't need to use the Sharingan to make sure. He sensed zero trace of genjutsu. It was simply a tidy lot.

In other words, there was no house.

For no particular reason, he looked up at the sky and saw two falcons circling high above. A mated pair, or maybe parent and child, seemingly without a care in the world, comfortably free.

Then came a voice from behind him. "Dad?"

He turned around to find his daughter, Sarada. Her eyes were wide beneath the bright red frames of her glasses.

"It's you." She gaped for a mere second before a smile spread across her face and she bounded toward him. Clenching both hands in front of her chest, she stared up at him intently. "You came back? When?"

"I happened to be near the village. I just got here."

"You did." Sarada smiled again and looked around them

before nodding toward the people coming and going. "I bet it's been a long time since you've seen so many people. You're not freaked out?"

He wasn't particularly bothered given that it hadn't actually been that long since he'd come home, thanks to the whole incident with Shin pretending to be an Uchiha. But in the face of Sarada's expectant gaze...

"Mm-hmm." Sasuke decided to assent.

"I knew it. And today's especially like a festival, so everyone's all worked up."

"A festival?"

"The Lord Seventh gave the holiday a name. Family Day." Sarada's voice grew excited at *family*. "I guess there's all kinds of events where families compete together. Like target shooting with shuriken, quick polishing kunai. I think there's even an eating contest. Hey! Did you want to stop in somewhere? Although I'm not so into the eating contest." She grinned, seemingly carried away by the festive mood of the town. Or else the unexpected reunion with her father was making her that way.

He didn't respond right away, but rather stared at the beaming face of his ever-changing daughter. Finally, as her expression relaxed into a slight smile, Sasuke pointed toward the empty lot behind them.

"Actually..." He sought an answer to his earlier question. "Where did the house disappear to?"

"Huh?" Her smile grew awkward. She looked at the empty lot and then back at her father's face. "Dad... What's with the joke? It's not very good, you know."

He frowned. "Joke?"

"Oh. You're serious." Her smile dropped away as though the strings holding up the corners of her mouth had been cut, and her face grew solemn. "It's true the house used to be here. But after Mom smashed it, it had to be rebuilt. We're staying in an apartment until it's done. And, like, we had supper together there, you know? How could you forget?"

Sasuke was at a loss for words. In the silence, the falcons above cried out and flew off, each in its own separate direction. "That…was a different place?"

"Sigh." Sarada put a hand to her brow and sighed, deeply. "Whatever. I'll show you the way to the apartment. Follow me." Without waiting for a reply, she turned on her heel and started walking.

Sasuke glanced at the empty lot and then silently followed his daughter.

"So basically, that's how long it's been since you were home," she remarked. "And you never tell us what you're doing out there, either."

They walked along a street lined with food stalls. Yellow, red, green—brightly colored banners flapped in the breeze, and balloons patterned after foods like bananas, apples, and tomatoes swayed alongside them. Everyone looked to be having a great time. All except his daughter. Her back radiated angry dissatisfaction.

And he couldn't exactly argue with her. He looked down at her sullen, shaking shoulders. "How about I buy you some candy?" he suggested.

"No thanks."

"Candy apples. They're red, you know."

"Why're you pushing red on me?" she snapped.

"You don't like red? I always assumed it was your favorite color." Sasuke had seen what his daughter wore, and that was the conclusion he'd come to.

"Well." She paused. "I don't *hate* red."

"So then how about tomatoes? There was a frozen tomato booth—"

"I *despise* tomatoes."

"You do?" At a loss for words again, Sasuke fell silent. He assumed that they would keep walking and take this awkward silence along with them, but then Sarada stopped abruptly.

"What's wrong?" he asked.

"You maybe got the Nine Tails Kuraa-ma?!"

A familiar voice reached his ears. Naruto.

"Yeah? Okay then. Thanks then!"

He turned his eyes in that direction just as Naruto flew out of the twenty-four hour shop, general store. The girl he carried on his back was…his daughter? She was squealing and laughing with delight. Naruto charged off toward another shop, apparently not noticing Sasuke. He shouted his question about Kuraa-ma again, and then he was off to a different store.

"What is that loser doing?" Sasuke was exasperated, but then he realized that Sarada was staring in the same direction, the happy father and daughter reflected hazily in the lenses of her glasses. This brought up another bout of nostalgia for him.

"Heh heh heh…"

"You laugh after twisting your ankle. Hey… You hitching a free ride?"

"No!"

He remembered that youthful day when Itachi had carried him on his back, remembered their conversation.

"Itachi, will you train with me again?"

"Sure… But I have missions, and you start at the academy tomorrow. So we probably won't have so much time together, just the two of us."

"That's okay…"

"As long as we can be together sometimes."

A laugh had slipped out as he lifted his face. His eyes were

at the same height as Itachi's, a fact that made him unbear-
ably happy. To be able to see the world in the same way as his
ever-distant brother...

Sasuke smiled faintly and turned his attention back to
Sarada. She was still staring at Naruto and his daughter with
a wistful and vaguely envious gaze.

"A piggyback...hm?" He touched her shoulder, gently.

"Huh? What?"

He turned his back to a baffled Sarada and crouched down.
He'd been able to read her feelings for the first time that day,
in the jealous gaze she turned on Naruto and his daughter.
And what she wanted at that moment wasn't a candy apple or
a frozen tomato. *This* was what she wanted.

However.

His back remained empty, free of any extra weight. He
looked back, questioningly, and met Sarada's eyes.

She stared down at him coldly. Then, without a single word,
she took a circuitous detour around him and walked away.

As she disappeared into the throng of people, Sasuke stood
up, alone. He cocked his head to one side ever so slightly.

@ @ @ @ @

The road he used to walk along as a child was now a large
river, the two sides joined by an arching bridge. Or maybe
this had always been a river, and he was mistaking it for a
different road, just as he'd completely forgotten the location of
the house.

Sasuke turned his gaze in the direction of Hokage Rock and
looked at the group of tall buildings that had sprung up there.
There was no need to chase after his daughter. He figured
he'd probably be able to find their apartment if he headed in

that direction. And if he was going that way anyway, then he ought to take a trip down memory lane and go down a road he used to walk all the time—no, naturally, this thought didn't occur to him. He merely selected a deserted back alley away from the hustle and bustle and happened upon the river. That was all.

He started over the bridge. Its slope was steep, making the bridge something that was more *climbed* than crossed. He squinted when the other side of the bridge came into view like the line of a mountain ridge.

A man was squatting there. Sasuke considered the possibility that he had gotten dizzy and, unable to keep going, had sat down on the spot. But that was clearly not it. The man was in a bunny-hop position, like he was lying in wait for someone to carry on his back.

Sasuke ignored the man and kept his distance as he walked around him to the other side, just like his daughter had done to him. He was about to continue on his way when…

"Oh dear," the man said, standing up smoothly. "I do think you should simply accept the kindness of other people."

Sasuke glared back over his shoulder at the man. "And exactly how is *that* kind?"

"Now, look. This old man here is trying to give you a piggyback, okay? When he's well on in years. Where else would that come from but a place of sheer kindness?"

It was the Sixth Hokage, Hatake Kakashi.

Sasuke hadn't seen him in quite some time, but the older man hadn't changed a bit. The only real difference from the old days was that he'd stopped hiding his left eye with his forehead band. His silver hair growing out in all directions and the detached look on his face were the same as always.

"Well, if you'd actually climbed on, I would've run away at full speed. Quite a sight to see there. Two old men piggybacking. Creepy *and* painful," Kakashi noted sarcastically.

Sasuke stared at him. "What are you doing here?"

"Hm? Oh, y'know, I just happened to catch sight of you." His former team leader laughed cheerfully. "The sad sack of a dad getting the cold shoulder from his daughter when he tried to give her a piggyback. So I came to tease you—no, I'm kidding. Don't glare at me like that."

"Hmph." Sasuke snorted his contempt.

Kakashi let out a short sigh. "You see me again for the first time in who knows how long, and you can't even be bothered to say hello? That's all you got? We could have a little ritual where we both rejoice in each other's good health." He twirled a finger around, as if searching for the right word. "Mm. Like a high five or something."

"No thanks." Sasuke started to move again, ignoring the hand held up before him. Kakashi set the hand down on Sasuke's shoulder, however, and Sasuke was forced to look back. "What? You still want something?"

"Hang on a sec. You know, you're really something. Maybe it's because you're always travelling alone, you've sure upped your antisocial skills. You ever actually talk to people?"

"I have conversations."

"With who?" Kakashi raised a doubtful eyebrow.

Sasuke looked back at him, expressionless, and fell silent. After a moment of deep thought, the answer came to him. "With Aoda."

"Aoda's a snake," Kakashi noted. "I didn't know I had to specify *people*."

"I guess his grandson's gotten longer lately. He talks about it with great joy," Sasuke said.

"Oh, is that right…" Kasashi rolled his eyes and redirected the conversation back to his original point. "No wonder things aren't going too well with your daughter."

Sasuke flinched, a single line popping up in the center of his brow. "What's that supposed to mean?"

"Just what I said. I was standing a ways off, but even still, the awkwardness came through loud and clear."

"All in your head. Sarada and I get along fine."

"And yet you tried to win her over with candy?" It seemed Kakashi had seen everything.

Sasuke clicked his tongue in reply.

"Well, you're not the worst, but we certainly can't call you World's Greatest Dad. You can talk to me if you want. How about it?"

"It's none of your business," Sasuke said thornily.

"Don't be like that." Kakashi smiled. "Oh, if you're worried about making trouble for me, no need for that. I've stepped down from my position as Hokage. And if it's time you're worried about, I've got more than I can handle."

"You're not actually worried about us, are you?" Sasuke said. "You're just bored."

"Aaah, so you got my number, huh?" Kakashi didn't look shy about it as he scratched the back of his head.

Before Sasuke could decide if that was the truth of the matter, Kakashi thrust a finger in his direction.

"But, you know, it's like, really *think* here and remember. There aren't too many people who can teach you anything."

"I suppose. Basically only Itachi and…that loser," he replied.

"Huh? Ohh, yeah," Kakashi said. "I guess so. And—"

"My father taught me Fire Style."

"Right, right. And—"

"And Orochimaru, I suppose."

"Him?"

"Although I suppose it's more accurate to say that I stole from him than that he taught me."

"What about Chidori? Hey!" Kakashi prompted, hopefully. "Maybe you should be remembering Chidori right about now."

"Aren't you single, anyway? I doubt you'd have any good advice."

Perhaps because Sasuke didn't so much as blink at the Chidori thing, Kakashi's half-lidded eyes narrowed even further. Then he pulled himself back together and said, "True. I don't have kids, so whatever you have to say about how hard it is to be a parent, I prob'ly won't really get it. But, you see...I've got my own ace up my sleeve." He puffed his chest up and pulled out a book.

"Is that..." *Exactly how many times is he going to reread it?*

The parts exposed to the light were faded to a snowy white, covered in dark finger-shaped smudges—outlining perhaps a palm—from when Kakashi held the book open with one hand. To an outsider, it looked like the very picture of an antique text.

"Make-Out Paradise."

"I treasure this book." Kakashi's voice grew stern, as if Sasuke sullied the volume in his hand by speaking its title so casually. "It's really an instruction manual for life, to be honest," he continued passionately.

In contrast, Sasuke was ready with the wet blanket. "Ridiculous."

"It's not ridiculous!" Kakashi raised his voice, likely not especially pleased about being shut down in a single word. "You want to be closer to your daughter, right? That's basically it, yeah? That sort of thing's called 'make-out.'"

"That sort of thing?"

"That sort of thing. Meaning I will impart to you now the secrets of the make-out. Now listen up. First, all right..."

@ @ @ @ @

Sasuke said goodbye to Kakashi and returned to the food-stall street jammed with people. He let his eyes roam the area. He had assumed it would be difficult to find a particular face in the dizzying crowd, but he did actually manage to find who he was looking for.

A girl in red squeezed through the surge of people and popped out ahead of him. It was Sarada.

"Oh! There you are!" Her glasses sat askew on her face, perhaps knocked out of place by a passerby. As she straightened them, she walked up to him, looking unhappy. "Honestly. I mean, come on. Don't just go disappearing! You're not a child."

Hands on her hips, she let out a deep sigh. "Well, it's my own fault for walking off without saying anything."

When Sasuke didn't react in any way, Sarada raised a curious eyebrow. "Dad?"

He didn't respond to this, either. As he stared into his baffled daughter's eyes, Sasuke was thinking about something entirely different. About what Kakashi had said.

"To you get closer, you gotta do something about what you call her. You know how you can give a person a fond nickname? You gotta do that for her. I mean, 'bro' feels a whole lot cozier than 'big brother.' Friendlier. You ever give anyone a nickname? Like, Sakura or—no, huh? I guess not… Well, you don't actually have to go out of your way at this point in the game, though. You shoulda been calling her some cute pet name right from the start if that's what you were gonna do. Like, how you call Naruto a loser? I think that's great, it has a real closeness to it… Hey. Why are you pulling that face? Anyway, try calling your daughter this for a start…"

"Peanut," Sasuke said, abruptly.

Sarada gave him a scowl in return. "Huh?"

But Sasuke paid this no mind. "You're my cute little peanut."

"What's with the monotone?" She raised an eyebrow at him.

Kakashi had read this line from one of the characters in *Make-Out Paradise* out loud to him (as Sasuke's face grew increasingly red) and told Sasuke to copy it, but of course, Sarada had no way of knowing that.

"And I'm not a legume," she noted.

He had only quoted one half of the couple's conversation, so naturally, this did not a conversation make.

No sooner had he learned that this pet name was pointless than he was immediately wiping the word *peanut* from his mind. Cursing the time he'd wasted, he turned to the next strategy Kakashi had offered up.

"And like..." Sarada's confusion changed to stiffness. "I mean, 'peanut'? Dad, you haven't said my name once yet today. Did you forget more than just where the house is? Did you seriously forget the name of your own daughter?" The words sounded as though they were intended as a joke, but her eyes weren't smiling at all.

"What are you talking about?" Sasuke's face was also smile-free as he responded in a flat tone. "It's Sarada."

"Huh. So you do remember. For now, anyway," she added, turning away.

Sasuke took off the overcoat he was wearing and slid it over her shoulders.

"What?" She looked up at him, confused. "I'm not actually cold or anything, you know."

"Just wear it."

Sarada furrowed her brow, apparently not understanding the meaning of this gesture.

This was another tactic Kakashi had pulled from *Make-Out Paradise*: a girl would always feel a thrill in her heart when a man's jacket was placed over her shoulders.

However.

"Oh my, how cute."

He heard a giggle from somewhere, and Sarada's shoulders jerked upward.

"Right? I suppose she wanted to wear it herself after she saw her father wearing it."

"But the size is a little… Right?"

Hearing the whispers of passersby, Sasuke looked down at his daughter, while she also looked down at herself. The baggy sleeves. The slumped shoulders. The coat had been made for Sasuke's height; it didn't fit Sarada's physique at all, making her look very sad indeed.

Without a word, Sarada removed the coat and threw it at her father. He accepted the coat without a fight.

On unsteady feet, she headed toward the sea of people she'd only just come out of. But she stopped as she was about to be swallowed up by the flow and looked back over her shoulder. "Dad, today you're, like…" Arrow-like eyes turned toward him, she spat, "Freaky."

◎　◎　◎　◎　◎

"Freaky, huh?" Kakashi laughed, delighted.

Sasuke, determined to ignore this, pretended not to hear his former master's laughter as he set his elbows down on the railing and stared down at the flowing river.

After Sarada had rejected him so obviously, he'd felt awkward about simply following her, and so he'd ended up back at the bridge. Waiting there for him, of course, was Kakashi's grinning face.

"Aah, kids, huh? No matter how awful it gets, she's still your daughter. Yup, that's how it is with families." Kakashi leaned back against the railing and peered at Sasuke's face, which made it hard to keep ignoring him.

"That book," Sasuke sighed and glanced at him out of the corner of his eye. "*Make* whatever. You still have it?"

"You can't just—It's *Make-Out Paradise*. Of course I have it. Why? You can't possibly... Have you awakened to the miracle that is *Make-Out Paradise* at long last?" Kakashi asked, grinning, perhaps excited about the birth of a new comrade.

Sasuke's response was immediate. "Give it here. I'll throw it in the river."

"Harsh." Sadly, Kakashi pulled back the hand that had been reaching into his pocket for the book. "Well, the stuff in *Make-Out Paradise* was written before your daughter was born. Might be a little dated. It'd totally trounce someone a bit older. At any rate," he sighed, discouraged. "If the stuff in *Make-Out Paradise* isn't working, then unfortunately, that's the end of it. I can't think of anything else you could do. I've gotten old too, after all."

"Maybe it's not the book I should throw in the river, Kakashi," Sasuke mused. "It's you."

"Not wrong there. You need to cool off a bit, too. How about we jump in together? We'll probably have thought up a great plan by the time we drift out to sea." However noble his words, Kakashi had absolutely no intention of actually getting wet. He closed his eyes and nodded. "Well, we can rack our brains till the end of time on this one, but an old man just can't understand how a child—how a *girl* feels. Be a lot simpler just to ask someone who has a daughter about this stuff, wouldn't it? Like Naruto."

This speech could also have been taken as a declaration of defeat.

"Not a chance." Sasuke shook his head. "He seems pretty busy."

"Hmm." Kakashi nodded thoughtfully. "It's true Naruto's maybe pushing himself a little too hard lately. Thanks to the growth in Konoha, even more people live in the village. So it makes sense that the burden on the Hokage would be greater than when I was Hokage—"

"No. That's not what I meant." Sasuke jerked his thumb toward the street with the food stalls. "I saw him running around with his own daughter."

"Naruto?" Kakashi opened his eyes wide, apparently taken by surprise with this news.

"Mm-hmm. It sounded like he was looking for Nine Tails. Can he have lost his Biju?"

"He'd be in a real tight spot if he had."

"He seemed to be okay, though." Question marks popped up above both their heads. "Well, if he's okay, then there's no issue, I suppose."

"If you can't talk to Naruto..." Kakashi hung his head and brought a hand to his chin. "Someone else who has a daughter... Kurenai? No." He swallowed the words he was about to say and snorted, his nose covered by his black mask. "There is one other person you could talk to."

Kakashi looked toward the other side of the bridge. Sasuke followed suit and saw what was likely a father and daughter about to cross. The father was a slender man with swirl marks on both cheeks. Sasuke felt like he had seen him somewhere before, but he couldn't quite place him. But he remembered the girl in tow. Dark brown skin and orange hair. She'd been with Sarada that day when Naruto came to Shikoro Pass.

"I *thought* I smelled potato chips, and just as I feared," Kakashi whispered in his ear while they waited for the pair to approach. Indeed, both father and daughter were eating potato chips. And they weren't even sharing one bag; they each had their own.

"Oh! Lord Sixth!" the father cried out, finally noticing them.

"And Sarada's dad!" the daughter added.

"Hey." Kakashi raised a hand in response. "I guess you're enjoying Family Day to the fullest. Sorry, you mind if I have one of those?"

"Huh? Oh. Sure. Of course." The father held the bag of chips out to Kakashi.

Where exactly have I seen him before? Sasuke dug through his memory, searching for a name. It was an extremely arduous task, but...

"I remember." He finally found the end of the thread. "Akimichi Choji. I didn't realize it was you. You've lost all that weight. You used to be much f—"

Fatter, he was going to say, but Kakashi tossed a potato chip into his open mouth before he could finish.

What is the meaning of this? he asked with his eyes.

Read the room, Kakashi answered, also with only his eyes.

Sasuke wanted to argue the point, but the potato chip sitting in his mouth was in the way. He would look silly if he simply let it sit there, so he chewed and swallowed.

Confusion rose up on Choji's face at the wordless exchange.

"Ha ha ha ha." Kakashi feigned a laugh to change the topic. "So the thing is? This guy wants to be closer to his daughter, so we've been sitting here thinking up ways to do that. But we're kind of at a dead end. And the two of you come along, just when we were talking about asking a mom or dad with a daughter the same age."

Choji blinked before he caught on. "I see. If you want to talk about being close with your daughter—"

"Couldn't you just eat potato chips together?" His own daughter crunched away on her chips.

"Right," Choji said, looking down at her. "Doesn't even have to be chips. Maybe you could just eat something delicious together." He stuffed some chips into his own mouth and exchanged a smile with his daughter. The grins plastered on their faces were almost identical.

Kakashi also smiled as he nodded in reply, but his face grew serious again when he turned back to Sasuke. "Hear that?"

Sasuke shrugged. They could tell him to go eat something tasty, but he had no idea of what Sarada liked. About all he knew was that she hated tomatoes.

"If we're talking about Sarada here" Choji said, bringing chips to his mouth between words, "Then I think there's someone better you could ask for advice."

Sasuke furrowed his brow doubtfully and exchanged a glance with Kakashi.

◎ ◎ ◎ ◎ ◎

Choji had told him where to go. And now Sasuke stood before the door alone, a finger pressed to the intercom.

He heard the airy sound of chimes, following by a voice from inside. "Coming!"

The door swung open, and a woman's face peeked out.

"Oh…" Her jaw dropped as she took in Sasuke, and the open door started to slowly close. But before it could close completely, she pulled it open again, all the way out until the door stopper caught and held it. But she kept her hand on it as she stared up at Sasuke's face. After a moment, she released the door with a gasp and took several hesitant steps backward to make space in the entryway.

"Welcome home, honey," Sakura said as she clasped her hands behind her back. A breeze blew in to ruffle her cherry-blossom pink hair.

"Mm, I'm back," Sasuke said for the first time in who knew how long. He had finally made his way home.

"Sarada told me you were in Konoha. But then you didn't come home… I was a bit worried." Sakura's voice tensed as she headed into the house.

"Things happened," he told her, unable to say he'd actually forgotten where they lived. "Is Sarada back then?"

"She came back for a bit, but then left again right away. She was angry about something. And here I thought we could finally all have dinner together for once."

"I see."

Sakura turned toward the kitchen, but Sasuke stopped in the living room in front of the display case. He looked down at the three framed photos there; a picture of his wife and daughter; a photo taken when he was a boy with Team Seven; and a picture of his wife, his daughter, and him.

The photographer had kept at him because it had been a while since he'd had his photo taken: "Dad, could you smile a bit more?" and "Bigger smile!" and "Like this, more natural…" and "Are your facial muscles dead?"

"Trip down memory lane?" Sakura came back with teacups on a tray. From her tone, it seemed that she had gotten the wrong impression, that he was looking at the picture of Team Seven.

"No. I was just staring into space." He accepted a cup and sipped at the tea before realizing Sakura was still looking at him, staring intently at his face.

"What?"

"Your hair's grown quite a lot."

He peered into the teacup and compared the face reflected in the tea with the one locked away in the picture frame. He did feel like his hair had indeed gotten longer since the photo shoot.

"How about I cut it for you?" she suggested.

"Oh—" He was about to refuse, but then gave up. "I guess so. Would you?"

"Got it. Just hang on a sec. I'll get the scissors."

He watched his wife disappear, humming quietly, before he returned his gaze to the framed photo. The expression on the face of Sarada was dignified.

"Dad, today you're, like...freaky."

It didn't bear the slightest resemblance to the look on her face when she spat out those words, disgusted.

"Okay, sit down."

When he turned around, he saw that a sheet had been spread out in the center of the living room and a chair placed in its center.

"Right." Sasuke took off his overcoat, rolled it up, and tucked it next to the photos before sitting down in the chair. A towel was quickly wrapped around his neck, so there was no real change in the way he looked.

"You want it long enough in the front on the left to cover your eye, right?" Sakura started to hum again and play with his hair. "Are you upset about Sarada? Is that it?"

Sasuke narrowed his eyes at the sudden question. "Did Kakashi call you?"

"No, but I can tell that much at least without anyone calling me. We're married, after all," Sakura added, in a quiet voice.

He was about to argue and started to look over his shoulder, but she pushed his head back. "Okay, don't move." He heard the sharp *snip* of the scissors immediately next to his ear and felt the bits of hair slipping down over the fabric.

"I'm not particularly upset," he said, facing forward since he had been given no other option.

"Really?"

Sasuke pursed his lips. He fumbled for what to say, but he couldn't decide on anything, so he said nothing.

"See?" Sakura smiled, faintly. "You *are* upset, aren't you?"

"I'm not upset—"

"Yes, yes. Don't move."

Now he heard the *snip* by his other ear.

Sasuke gave up, words half frozen in his mouth, and sank into silence.

"It would be so much easier if we could just chalk it up to her being at 'that rebellious age,'" Sakura said, pulling a comb through his hair. "But I think with that girl, she really adores her dad, more than your average kid. And she doesn't get to see you very much, so she builds you up in her mind. You're cooler than other dads, you're stronger than other dads. Although I guess that's actually true!"

She laughed, sounding embarrassed at how lovey-dovey this came across.

"When she catches just a glimpse of a less-than-great thing about you, she's all the more disillusioned. Nothing to be done there, honestly. You give her so much to wrestle with." She slowly brushed away the hair that had fallen on his shoulders. "Sarada still has no idea what you're really like. I think you just have to be normal with her and not act all big and tough. As for what specifically you should do… Well, I don't really know that either."

The hand brushing his shoulder slowly came to a stop as Sakura continued, "Doesn't she just want what you wanted from your father when you were a kid?"

◎ ◎ ◎ ◎ ◎

Sarada readied her shuriken on the bank of the river flowing through the forest. A little farther downstream, the river reached a cliff, and the roar of the waterfall enveloped her. The water flow at the source was violent, twisting, forceful enough to smash stones. White foam rose up on the surface.

And knocked about by this vortex was a target, a double circle. She had tossed the log bearing the target into the river after tying it to a nearby tree. It was impossible to predict the movement of such a target, making it ideal for shuriken training.

She readied her weapon and threw it.

Shff!

But the shuriken wildly missed its mark and plunged into a tree on the opposite bank.

"Aah! Come *on*!" Sarada cried out in irritation. Several shuriken were already embedded in the trees. "Why can't I *do* this?"

But she knew the reason only too well. She took several deep breaths to calm herself.

"Okay!"

She threw another shuriken. This time, it spun directly toward the center of the target, as though sucked in somehow. Sarada held her breath.

However.

Klang!

Before her weapon could hit the target, another shuriken knocked it away.

Sarada dropped down into a ready stance, prepared to fight the sudden intruder. But as soon as she saw the shrub that had thrown the shuriken, she stood up again, unamused. "What? Could you not get in my way, please?"

The one who had thrown the shuriken was…Sasuke. He came out from behind the shrub silently to stand alongside her.

She eyed him doubtfully, but eventually decided to ignore him and turned back toward the target on the water. She flung another shuriken.

Klang!

Once again, Sasuke's shuriken blocked it right before it could hit the bull's-eye.

"Hey!" she yelled.

Glancing at her out of the corner of his eye, Sasuke got the target in his sights and tossed a shuriken toward it.

"Ah!" Sarada cried out and threw her own shuriken.

Kakink!

This time, it was her shuriken that knocked his out of the air.

"Yes!" She struck a pose, as triumphant as if she had hit the center of the target. But when she realized that Sasuke was watching her, she turned her back to him, awkwardly.

He couldn't keep a slight laugh from slipping out. "Sakura told me," he said, readying his next shuriken. "She said you want to be Hokage."

Sasuke had thought it was the father and daughter together that had captured Sarada's envy when they saw Naruto and his daughter on the street with the food stalls. But he had misunderstood. Sarada hadn't been staring at Naruto the father, but at Naruto the Hokage.

"What, you gonna laugh and tell me it's a hopeless dream?"

"Nah." Sasuke shook his head. "I tried to become Hokage once, too."

"What?" Sarada froze in surprise, and Sasuke took the opportunity to throw his shuriken.

Quickly recovering herself, his daughter hurriedly tossed her own shuriken. The two weapons slammed into each other and fell into the river with a sharp metallic *klank*.

"That's the first I've heard of that," she said, finally.

"I only told a few people. I wanted to announce it formally, but the time and place were always bad." As was the ideology he'd clung to then.

Before he could tell her that part, Sarada swiftly launched a shuriken. She was secretly trying for the target.

Skreeenk!

Once again, two shuriken disappeared into the river.

Tch! Sarada clicked her tongue.

Sasuke narrowed his eyes and raised the corner of his mouth ever so slightly. Just the tiniest amount. He intended to smile, but perhaps it came across as a sneer to Sarada. She sniffed in annoyance.

But this too was only for an instant.

She chuckled with self-satisfaction and raised her right hand. Pinched between her fingers, three shuriken glittered a dark grey. In the next instant, she threw all three simultaneously. The shuriken arced toward the target.

Klank! Krk! Skreenk!

"Huh?!"

Her three shuriken were knocked out of the air without exception by Sasuke's. And just one throw, one shuriken.

She stared at him in disbelief.

Sasuke looked down on his daughter. "Hmph." This time, he laughed with his nose, rather than giving her a faint smile.

That was the signal to start.

She closed her eyes and slowly turned back toward the target. When she opened them again, her eyes were red. The Sharingan she'd inherited from her father.

"If it's a contest you want…" She crossed her arms in front of her chest. He didn't know where she'd gotten them from, but her hands were full, clutching shuriken. "Let's go all the way here!"

Swinging her arms as if scooping up weapons from the ground, Sarada launched her first shuriken at the target. She then swung her arms again and shot off another, and another—a succession of shuriken.

Sasuke casually knocked the endless hail of shuriken down into the river as though he were brushing aside a fly.

"The Hokage that I was aiming to be," he said, as metal clanged endlessly against metal, "was twisted."

"Shut up! You'll distract me!" Sarada shouted back, her hands in constant motion.

But Sasuke continued. "I had a friend, though, who warned me it was twisted. He walked ahead and showed me the correct path."

"What are you even on about? Are you boasting you used to be bad in the old days? Or about your friendship?!"

"He's not the kind of friend you boast about. He's just a loser who charges forward in whatever direction he thinks is him."

"I don't even understand what you're saying!"

"You were staring at his back," Sasuke said. "You won't mistake the path like I did. I'm sure you'll make a wonderful Hokage."

"Huh?" Sarada was stunned.

"I'm rooting for you. Don't give up."

She gaped, her mouth hanging open, perhaps unable to believe that he would give her any real encouragement.

And then the last shuriken she'd thrown was knocked off in an unexpected direction and severed the rope tied to the target. In an instant, the log was swallowed up by the swirling water and began to drift toward the waterfall.

"Ah!" she murmured regretfully, and let the hand clutching a shuriken slowly slide down.

"You're giving up?" Sasuke asked, and her hand froze in place.

She looked back to meet his eyes, and then grinned boldly. "Don't be stupid." She turned back toward the mouth of the waterfall and readied her shuriken once more.

Just as her Sharingan caught sight of the edge of the cliff, the target was tossed from the waterfall up into the air. She didn't let her chance get away.

The shuriken she flung forward headed toward the target with a bit of a curving trajectory. But the log was dropping faster than her weapon was moving, and she just barely missed. Sarada bit her lip in frustration.

Shf! Sasuke launched his own shuriken from behind her. With incredible speed, it chased after his daughter's and knocked it down toward the basin of the waterfall.

Shhkonk! They heard the sound of wood being hit.

Sarada was dumbfounded, but when she finally recovered herself, she raced to the edge of the cliff. Sasuke followed, and, standing alongside his daughter, he looked down toward the base.

Far below, a shuriken was firmly planted in the center of the target that bobbed up in the basin of the waterfall.

"Dad, that was amazing," she said, stunned, forgetting their fight.

"That wasn't me. It was your shuriken that hit the bull's-eye," he retorted, which seemed like splitting hairs, and Sarada frowned. But a grin soon spread across her face and the tension ran out of her shoulders.

Sasuke looked down on his daughter and her carefree smile, and his own lips curved upward, slightly. In his head, his wife's voice echoed: *Doesn't she just want what you wanted from your father when you were a kid?*

When she had said that to him, he'd felt again that burst of nostalgia he'd experienced standing in front of the empty lot. A boy still shedding his baby fat, desperately seeking something—*anything*—from his father. Trying to live up to his expectations so that he would say those magic words: *That's my boy.*

As he remembered how he had felt all those years ago, Sasuke wanted to give his own daughter that gift.

"That's my—"

Well, he *tried* to give her that gift. But then he hesitated. Hitting a target with a shuriken felt too small for such powerful words. There had to be something else he could say. Or else when she achieved something *really* big...

Sarada was looking at him curiously, perhaps because he'd suddenly gone silent. But the grin quickly returned to her face, and she took the long way around to getting him to spoil her a little. "Aaah. I get so hungry after training. Maybe you could get me something sweet. Like candy apples."

However.

Her smile withered when she looked up at her father's face again. She knew what was next. "Are you leaving already?"

"Mm-hmm. I just stopped by Konoha to file my mission report. I wasn't planning to stay long."

"You weren't?" his daughter mumbled. "So when are you going to come report again?"

"No idea," he replied artlessly, and then flapped the sleeves of his overcoat loudly as he turned on his heel. He could sense that Sarada still had something to say behind him, but he started to walk toward the woods. And then he heard her sniffling and his feet stopped.

He looked back to see her hurriedly removing her glasses and rubbing her eyes. He crossed again the distance he had only just covered and put a finger to his daughter's forehead.

She glared up at him with hard eyes. "You gonna try to smooth it over by jabbing me in the forehead again?"

His hand froze.

What was this about a jab? Although the thought had perhaps crossed his mind.

He slid his hand off to one side and touched her eyebrow. "It's not a jab." He bent down and brought his eyes to her level. "It's Fire Style."

"Next time I come home, I'll teach you Fire Style," Sasuke said, squarely meeting his daughter's eyes.

She seemed uncertain, but when a grin spread across her father's face, she smiled back, brightly.

4 MASTER SHINO! AND THE DEMANDING PARENT?

Working as a teacher, the only people he really spoke with were students—nothing but children. He did talk with other adults occasionally, however. He had colleagues, superiors, workers who came and went at the academy. And…

"Mm."

"Hmm."

As Shino walked along Konohagakure's main street, he noticed someone coming directly toward him, and his feet stopped. The other man also stopped. Facing each other there, the first words they said were "Mm" and "Hmm." Shino was "Hmm."

Speaking with adults meant colleagues. Superiors. Workers. And…

"Uchiha Sasuke."

His students' parents. Shino faced Sasuke.

"Aburame Shino."

Whenever his former student Uchiha Sarada had needed a guardian with her for whatever reason, it had always been her mother, Sakura. Since becoming an instructor at the academy, Shino had never had the chance to speak with Sasuke. In fact, he hadn't really had the chance before he became a teacher, either.

Had he ever really spoken with Sasuke in his chunin or genin days—or even back when he was a student himself? He went back through his memories, but all he found were a few words exchanged when Orochimaru attacked Konoha in front of Kankuro from Sunagakure.

Shino stared vacantly, lost in this reverie, until he came to a single conclusion.

I have no idea what I'm supposed to say to him.

Sasuke likely felt the same. While Shino turned his head up toward the sky, Sasuke stared at the ground.

However.

"So." Surprisingly, it was Sasuke who set the conversation in motion. "I heard you were my daughter's teacher at the academy."

"Oh. Mm-hmm." Shino straightened up, conscious of their relationship as instructor and student's parent. He cleared his throat. "The path she wants to travel's definitely not an easy one. It will likely be difficult, a harsh journey. I hope you'll do what you can to help. As her father."

"As her father..." A pensive look came across Sasuke's face, as if this were already something he'd been mulling over. "Then...perhaps I should I ask you. As a father." He brought a hand to his chin. "...creepy insects?"

"What was that?" Shino hadn't quite caught the question. He concentrated, listening carefully to Sasuke's reply.

"She hasn't picked up any weird hangers-on, no creepy insects?"

This time, he caught it. He caught it loud and clear. He held his tongue and looked back up at the sky, though not because he was trying to remember something again. No, he needed to stare at the endless blue and try to calm himself down. Although the blue was quite dull because he was seeing it through

his goggles.

Shino envisioned the word *patience* there. Just once wasn't enough. He wrote it twice and then three times. *Patience, patience, patience...* He started to doubt that the letters *p-a-t-i-e-n-c-e* really spelled the word, so he tried writing it in cursive. *Patience.*

A ninja was someone who persevered, who had patience. There was nothing they couldn't handle. But his body started to shake despite this resolve.

"Th-there—!" And now, even his voice was shaking. "There are no creepy insects!!"

A swarm of bugs casually devoured the words Shino had written above his head.

EPILOGUE

The following day, after Family Day had ended more or less without incident, Naruto sat down on his chair in the Hokage's office and let out a long sigh. Leaning his head back against the chair, he stared vacantly up at the ceiling. The familiar ceiling. For some reason, he felt like he was seeing it now for the first time in a long time, even though he'd only been away one day. Maybe it was because he'd only been staring down at his desk lately.

He heard footsteps approaching in the hallway, a sound he was also familiar with. Shikamaru.

"You just had a day off. What's that look for?" Shikamaru said with a wry smile when he opened the door.

Naruto stroked his cheek. "Do I have a weird look on my face?"

"It's got 'worn out' written all over it. Didn't you get any rest?"

"I was running around the whole day." Naruto moved his hand down to the back of his neck. "That's probably it."

"That so?" Shikamaru smiled again and closed the door.

"What about you? You actually get any time off?"

"Nah, not a bit. In fact, not only did I not get time off, I was nearly killed by dumplings."

"Dumplings…?" Naruto assumed this was some kind of joke, but Shikamaru was serious.

"On top of that, Temari flipped out on me when I got home, all 'How dare you come home after losing?!' Super scary. She nearly killed me, too. My day off was this close to being the day of my death," Shikamaru muttered, also looking extremely tired.

"But, you know," he continued, quietly, casually. "I guess it wasn't a bad day off. Better than the ones where I just go home to sleep. Right?"

"Yeah," Naruto replied, with an ear-to-ear grin. "Not only was it not too bad… It was the best day off. Believe it. It'd almost be great if we could do it once a month."

The corners of Shikamaru's mouth turned up ever so slightly. "In that case, I got some good news for you." *Fwup!* He tossed a stack of papers onto the desk.

"What's this?" Naruto looked up, puzzled.

"Petitions. Arrived this morning. Basically—" Shikamaru started, but was interrupted by voices outside.

And it wasn't simply people chatting. A large crowd had gathered below the Hokage's window, and they were shouting loudly.

Naruto and Shikamaru exchanged a doubtful look and approached the window.

"W-what is *that*?" the Hokage gasped.

People thronged before the office. As many as at Masuda the day before—no, even more than that.

Naruto popped his head out the window, and individual voices became clear among the noise of the crowd.

"It's not fair! I mean, only families?!"

"Exactly! What about Couples' Day? And we should have Sisters' Day, too!"

"We need Singles' Day! Some kind of thing where single people come together and talk to each other about hobbies and income and future plans..."

"That's a matchmaking event! What we *really* need is Brothers' Day!"

Every single person there had their own individual demands.

"You all need to quiet down! Couples, brothers! Please! Enough of that! You can see all of them whenever you want! What we *actually* need is Grandfather and Grandchildren Day! We have to have a holiday for all the old men who never get to see their grandchildren!!" a man shouted in a remarkably large voice. A remarkably large man. Akimichi Choza.

And...maybe it was just in his head. But hidden behind this massive frame, Naruto thought he saw his father-in-law, Hyuga Hiashi, also shouting about Grandfathers' Day.

"It's gotta be Dogs' Daaaay!" Kiba yelled, trying very hard not to make eye contact. "You have to make a Dogs' Daaaaay!!"

"*That's* what's in the petitions," Shikamaru said, behind him. "So? You gonna do one a month?" He challenged the Hokage with his gaze

For a few moments, Naruto was simply dumbfounded. Then he laughed and pulled out his Hokage seal. "So it was couples and sisters and brothers...and then grandfathers and grandchildren and dogs, right?"

Family Day had indeed strengthened the bonds between parents and children. But sisters, couples, and all the other people with their own special relationships deserved the same chance. The important thing was not a name on the calendar, but spending time together and getting the chance to really talk. If they had that, they could make it through even the most difficult of duties.

"Welp! Let's go wild! We'll give names to all the holidays! Believe it!" Naruto brandished his seal high in the air.

Masashi Kishimoto

ABOUT THE CREATOR

Author/artist Masashi Kishimoto was born in 1974 in rural Okayama Prefecture, Japan. After spending time in art college, he won the Hop Step Award for new manga artists with his manga *Karakuri* (Mechanism). Kishimoto decided to base his next story on traditional Japanese culture. His first version of *Naruto,* drawn in 1997, was a one-shot story about fox spirits; his final version, which debuted in *Weekly Shonen Jump* in 1999, quickly became the most popular ninja manga in Japan.

MIREI MIYAMOTO

ABOUT THE AUTHOR

Under the name Zoncho, Mirei Miyamoto won
the Jump Novel Grand Prix Summer '14 in the
character novel division. His work includes
Marunouchi of the Dead and *Tagayasu Zombie-sama*,
and he is always pushing himself in new directions
of storytelling, such as with his contribution to
Thus Spoke Kishibe Rohan: A Short Story Collection.